Spirit Wolf

A High Plains Warrior Novel

BY

Michael O. Gibbs

Spirit Wolf

A HIGH PLAINS WARRIOR NOVEL

ISBN-13: 978-1533108067
ISBN-10: 1533108064

Author: Michael O. Gibbs

For permission, please contact:
Michael O. Gibbs
highplainswarriornovel@gmail.com
www.highplainswarrior.com

Cover design by Kari Cureton

Book layout/design by David Larson

DEDICATION

To the Native Americans of North America who thrived here in the 1750s, and whose marvelous array of individual characters and fascinating adventures can only be imagined.

To the native wildlife of North America—with us to this day—which also has a marvelous array of individual characters and fascinating adventures.

To all the wonderful books I've read, both fiction and non-fiction, about human culture and animal behavior.

To David Larson (*The last Jewish Gangster, WEST, Mr. Meeks and many others)* whose constant encouragement and help drove me to start and finish this novel; to J.D. Wallace (*SILENT CATS: DEADLY DANCE*), whose professional skills and sharp commentary helped me beyond measure; to Jennifer Donohue (*The Fated*), who found every inappropriate word usage and character blunder I made—and there were many; and, to Marla Anderson (*NanoMorphosis*), who found every error—period.

1

Tall Rabbit had long been an outsider among his adopted people. His lodge, more an accumulation of propped-up, shabby castaway skins than a real teepee, was always filthy. He walked about muttering craziness rather than speaking to others, stole food from his neighbors—sometimes their dogs—and he marked the area surrounding his lodge in the same way wolves mark their territory.

For more than ten years, ever since he'd wandered into their camp as a starving, near-death nine-year-old, the strange young male relied upon the goodwill of the Wolf Ridge people. He steadfastly refused to take on the productive role of either a man or a woman and remained unresponsive to every attempt to draw him into the social fabric of their band.

Then today he had betrayed all trust in unexplained craziness—he murdered one of the villagers who took him in.

Wolf Ridge Elders could not remember a time when one band member had slain another, but today's great tragedy changed that. And it forever changed the lives of those closest to the murdered warrior, especially, his son, Lion Hunter.

The warrior, Fox Belly, was clubbed to death and his wife, Crow Woman, was forcibly dragged away to the killer's hovel. By nighttime, Crow Woman was rescued and the killer condemned to banishment, but no social issue involving the odd Tall Rabbit had ever been resolved that simply.

So now, long after the day's calamitous events, beneath the brooding pallor of a wane moon, both Tall Rabbit and the village site were abandoned. He would remain, inside of a lashed-down sweat lodge, tricked into believing his spirit was being cleansed while the Wolf Ridge people quietly packed their possessions and prepared to sneak off in the dead of night, in search of a new village site far away from the killer's sickened spirit.

By custom, his name would never be spoken again among them—he was forever dead to those who, in the past, had so willingly made themselves his keepers.

* * *

Shadowy figures scurried about, extinguished lodge fires, dismantled teepees and loaded packhorses. First wives snapped out whispered orders, dogs whined and horses whinnied with apprehension over the unusual nighttime commotion.

Crow Woman, mutely dismantling her murdered husband's teepee, forced herself to stop, lifted her chin to the late night breeze and stood, taut muscles shaking as she stared off into the blackness of the surrounding plain. After a moment, still twisting the shell necklace at her throat, she looked sideways at her son.

"Hunter," she said to the tall fifteen-year-old, while gesturing toward her dead husband's picketed camp pony. "Go to the village herd and get four more of your father's finest ponies. Picket them here with his camp pony."

Both watched as the dark form of the skittish pony shied away from her pointing finger, yanking at its tether and prancing.

"We will go to Kills-In-The-Dark and gift the ponies to her before the camp's move tonight."

"Go," she repeated when he failed to respond. The young brave looked to his mother, his dark eyes showing astonishment.

Why would you do such a thing, Mother? The little white-nose is my father's best war mare. And four more besides it…?

Lion Hunter's mind, heavy with the tragic effect of his father's slaying, struggled to grasp the significance of his mother's demand. That and the baffling presence of several women milling about his family's campsite, guardedly touching and discussing in whispers the various items from his father's lodge that had already been laid out by his mother.

Abruptly, his stomach knotted.

It is because my father is dead! We no longer own the things of my father's lodge.

The piecing together of these two bleak facts flooded understanding into his consciousness, and anguish closed in upon him.

All of our property will be taken. We will not even have the white-nose pony that was to be mine this coming winter.

Numb, Lion Hunter searched the shadowed features of his mother's face. She came to him, tenderly pushing several wind-blown strands of his long black hair aside, and took his thin face between her callused hands. It was an act she had avoided, although sadly, since his twelfth winter—a mother's gesture of respect for her son's coming manhood.

"You are a fine young brave, and soon you will go upon your vision quest and become a man. But you are still my precious son, and you must do as I ask one last time. No time has been so important to you as this."

Picking up a braided halter, she pressed it into his hand. He felt its coarse horsehairs pricking his flesh as her distant words snaked through his stormy emotions.

"I will finish taking apart our lodge and laying out these things for tonight's 'Taking.' Go now. Do as I have asked." The torture in her voice urged him to comply.

Lion Hunter turned, willing first one foot then the other to move toward the horse pasture. He did not understand why his mother wanted to take five ponies to the holy man's hideous wife—the camp's macabre medicine woman. A jumble of ominous thoughts invaded his mind, the most fearsome of which were those of the medicine woman herself. Her name, Kills-In-The-Dark, was only part of the strangeness that haunted those of her village—especially the young. Her right eye was milky-white with blindness—one malady among many resulting from the terrible beatings inflicted upon her during three years of captivity among the Blackfeet.

Lion Hunter's thoughts conjured the grisly image of her destroyed face, its skin riven with scar tissue pulling tautly at twin black slits in the center of her face where a nose should have been. Chill bumps washed over his forearms as he remembered her shudder-provoking scowl, a gesture she invariably greeted him, and others, with during chance encounters in and around the village. It was an utterly silent gesture with no conversation to soften its raw impact upon him.

* * *

"Why do you touch my father's ponies?" Lion Hunter demanded on finding a group of pasture boys separating and examining several of the animals.

Fuming, he waded in amongst the youngsters haltering a large black gelding they'd cut from the herd. Then, dropping the long lead to drag along the ground behind drove it and three others away from the group with sharp slaps to their haunches. Once free of the rest of the herd, he caught up the gelding's lead with his foot, swung up to the animal's broad back, and herded the others back toward his father's lodge. While still close enough to see in the pale moonlight, he glanced back and uncomfortably watched as the pasture boys returned to cutting out and inspecting the remaining horses, which so recently had belonged to his father.

As he rode up, his mother removed the last of the buffalo hides from the teepee's frame. She nodded silently to him, gesturing with her chin toward the wooden skeleton that remained. Without further direction, Lion Hunter pulled the poles down and bundled them for travel. Several neighboring women dawdled nearby, lingering but avoiding eye contact. He dreaded what would come next.

Among his people all property belonged to the warrior of the lodge. His father's death released his property to the people of his band. It now belonged to whatever lodge might need it most. Once he and his mother finished laying out the lodge's buffalo skins, poles, tools, and other family items, the dark figures lurking nearby would quickly pick through them, taking what they wished before vanishing into the night to finish breaking down their own lodges for the unprecedented late night move.

Under less urgent circumstances, the transfer of property would have been concluded in a more respectful ceremony. Over a two-day period, Lion Hunter and his mother could have expected invitations to various lodges to feast and consider offers of becoming extended family members around this, or that, new campfire—protected and cared for by a different warrior, one skilled enough to welcome two additional mouths to his lodge.

Lion Hunter remembered the camp storyteller sitting long ago at the village fire telling the camp's children the tale of Sun Boy who allowed his heat to be Taken so all of the Great Maker's people could survive the bitter winters of the Northern Plains—the need of the many greater than that of the few. The Taking custom also encouraged surviving family members to accept offers of refuge from other lodges.

But this camp movement was different, more urgent. And the fact that no other lodge had offered to take in Crow Woman, or her son, uprooted the custom. His mother was a Crow woman abducted during war and forced to become wife to his father. The Crow were enemy to the only people Lion Hunter had ever known—the Wolf Ridge people—his people. Some in the band had befriended his mother over the fifteen years she lived among them, but most simply tolerated her presence as long as her respected husband still lived. Lion Hunter's true heritage, rarely spoken of in the distant past, had been questioned in whispered conversations around the camp in recent years. Was he truly of Fox Belly's seed or was he Crow, already alive in his mother's belly when his father took her captive? There were no customs for these social shames. They just were.

Even Crow Chaser, his father's lifelong and closest friend, had not sent word of his willingness to take in Lion Hunter and his mother. His old hag of a wife certainly had her say in the matter of permanently admitting outsiders to his lodge.

From the possessions laid out for the Taking, Crow Woman gathered an extra pair of moccasins, Lion Hunter's leggings, fire starting kit and, as an afterthought, a buckskin shirt decorated with the soft winter coat of a mountain sheep on its arms and back. She stuffed the collected items into a pack she'd set aside for him, saving the shirt until last. She snuggled the shirt to her cheek briefly before slipping it into the pack with the other items.

Motioning for Lion Hunter to bring the gathered horses, she picked up the pack and resolutely tramped off into the night. For herself, his mother took only the dress and moccasins she wore. Lion Hunter collected his weapons and took up his father's war pony's lead—the others would follow.

Following his mother's shadowed form, Lion Hunter glanced back one last time at the former site of his father's lodge. New shadows emerged from the surrounding darkness as other villagers came to pick through and take ownership of the property that had once belonged to Fox Belly—respected warrior, husband and father, now dead, and as with all the dead, nameless to the Wolf Ridge people.

Lion Hunter's apprehension mounted as he quickened his pace, closing the distance between himself and his fast-moving mother.

Are we to be abandoned like the slayer who has stolen my father's life? Lion Hunter clutched the medicine bag hanging around his neck—dread saturating his fifteen-year-old heart.

Crow Woman stopped before a modest lodge on the outskirts of the band's encampment. Unlike the rest of the camp, activity going on around it was not evident. Clearly, its occupant did not feel rushed by the impending village move. Standing just outside the teepee's entrance Crow Woman called out to its occupant.

"Hey ya, medicine woman. It is I, Crow Woman. I wish to ask a kindness of you."

Long, silent moments followed. She called out a second time.

"Kills-In-The-Dark, I would speak of something much important to my son, Lion Hunter."

More silence. Still she waited.

Finally, rustling sounds came from inside, and the entrance flap jerked aside. The occupant's shadowed face came into view, glowering first at Lion Hunter's mother, and then, far longer, directly into Lion Hunter's eyes. The woman's one good eye was obsidian black and, even in moonlight, appeared maddened with intensity. Lion Hunter took an involuntary step backward. She did not have to scowl—the ugliness was permanent to her mutilated face.

Long silent moments passed before she moved aside, jerking a disfigured hand in a curt gesture for them to enter. Lion Hunter had never before noticed the two missing fingers on that hand. Perhaps it was because she had so many mutilations, or maybe because he always turned his eyes away whenever their paths chanced to cross.

Dark forebodings rising, Lion Hunter lashed his father's war pony to the picket pole alongside a pinto already secured there. The other four ponies herded up nearby.

Taking a deep breath, he bent and followed his mother into the fearsome lair of the woman village children called "witch." He had many times overheard whispered accounts of human skulls, evil hexes, and eerie whimpers in the night associated with her lodge, but none of those tales prepared him for what he found at the center of her lodge, prominently displayed above its glowering fire pit.

That traditional place of honor held five gruesome trophies dangling askew from a horsehair braid anchored to a lodge pole high overhead.

Not skulls, but real human heads—heads with grotesquely desiccated skin. Heads whose vacant eye sockets brooded down over their medicine woman mistress. Heads whose shriveled, starkly painted faces mutely bespoke the torment of human spirits trapped between the real and the spirit worlds—two white, one cobalt blue, the others black with yellow flaps of ears.

"Sit," the witch commanded of her horrified guests. They sat, the thick smell of musty herbs and smoldering sage closing in on them. But overpowering all was the lodge's dark necromancer, Kills-In-The-Dark—hunched and sinister—now sitting cross-legged before them.

Crow Woman gawked openly at the ghoulish war trophies. Lion Hunter, resisting the urge to scoot closer to his mother, sat stock still enduring the medicine woman's unnerving one-eyed glare.

"The Taking has begun," Lion Hunter's mother croaked before clearing her throat as she set aside the pack she'd prepared for her son. "We have no offer of shelter… I will go." While speaking she also used sign.

Time, now. Journey, there. She swept her arm toward the open plains, her face full of loss. She continued.

"But my son needs a lodge and a warrior to teach him to become a fine warrior for his people."

"And what is this to me?" the medicine woman asked with a growl.

"I ask that you remember the gift of kindness given to you by my husband many years past when you first returned from being a slave among the Blackfeet." Lion Hunter's father had taken pity on the emaciated and hideously mutilated nineteen-year-old newly returned to the Wolf Ridge camp with no remaining family. He had given her a buffalo skin to use as emergency shelter and continued providing her with food. And she survived beside the band for a year before finally agreeing to be taken in by the holy man, Ghost Head, first as his helper and eventually as his wife. Even then she remained a bitter, solitary woman who occupied a teepee aside from that of her husband.

"So, I ask that you honor his kindness by now taking in his son."

Stone silence.

"And we have brought five ponies to gift to you," she said, gesturing in the direction of nervous horse movements that could be heard outside.

Lion Hunter sat calamity-struck. *Must I live with this witch? Why am I not dead?*

Kills-In-The-Dark sat motionless, again fixing Lion Hunter with her unnerving one-eyed stare. Quickly shifting his own eyes away, his notice fell upon its milk-eyed companion floating like a new moon amid the canyons of her destroyed face. Again his eyes fled, this time to the black shadows beyond the fearsome woman. Then, abruptly annoyed by this act of fear, he pushed away the shock of his helplessness and forced himself to stare defiantly back at his new tormentor. But no amount of rebellious courage could bring him to look at the gruesome twin cavities at the center of her face, where once a nose had existed.

Eventually her good eye squinted, and a barely detectable smirk crept over the unfortunate ruin of her face.

"I accept the ponies, but tell me why I should accept this boy into my care?"

Insult stabbed at Lion Hunter's ego.

I will have no more insults from this ugly witch! He sprang to his feet, making to leave. He was a Wolf Ridge brave, well taught in the ways of the warrior by both his father and by the great warrior chief, Owl Eyes, his father's twin brother. That both had since been slain did not change the skills he earned through long hours of training and practice under their coaching.

"Boy!" the medicine woman barked. "Do you see these Blackfeet heads?" she asked pointing to the macabre knot of war trophies dangling overhead. "They are taken by *my* hand. Their spirits are slave to me for no reason but the anger their before-owners brought to me. Do not annoy me with your youthful moodiness. Now, sit!"

Lion Hunter sank to his haunches, yielding that much, silently acknowledging not only the woman's formidable power over him but also the helplessness of his current station among the only people he had ever known.

His mother would go into voluntary exile, the custom for a woman whose lodge and protector were no more. She would wander the wilderness in solitude, fated to mourn the loss of her husband and son through privation and self-mutilation until death at last released her spirit to the next world.

But mourning was forbidden to Lion Hunter, as it was to all men of his people. It was the duty of all Wolf Ridge men to become the best warriors they could, to sacrifice their lives if necessary, in providing for and protecting their people.

"Why should I accept this boy into my lodge?" the witch repeated to his mother.

"It is a kindness that I ask, for a boy who, from this time, has no family. There is nothing more to offer." Her statement penetrated his dejection, crashing through his thoughts like a raging summer storm.

Kills-In-The-Dark hunched over even more, gazing silently down into the coals of her fire for a lengthy period before responding in her strange hoarse voice.

"I will do this thing," she said, abruptly looking up at Crow Woman. "You go now."

Crow Woman rose immediately—her boy was safe. She picked up the pack and set it in Lion Hunter's lap, then turned to leave the teepee. When her hand gently touched his shoulder, Lion Hunter also began to rise but stopped short and sat at the medicine woman's renewed command, "You sit, Boy. Do not move."

Heartbroken, Lion Hunter stopped short, then silently sat down, his eyes fixed on the disfigured woman across from him. They listened to the sounds of his mother padding softly off into the night.

"I have slain these five enemies," she said, pointing her mutilated hand overhead without averting her fierce gaze. "And more," she added, making the stark pronouncement without explanation.

Lion Hunter, mentally stumbling out of the darkness of his confused emotions, refocused his eyes. He glanced at the macabre trophies indicated by her gesture, then looked back to the mysterious and frightening woman before him.

"I curse their names to the spirit world each day," her rough voice continued, "so that their spirits may never cross that way. I am the evil they have shaped with their doings and the terror their spirits will forever suffer for those doings."

"Know well that I am a warrior," she continued, unabashedly using the term reserved to describe successful men among their people. "I am savage and deadly, even beyond this world." For long moments thereafter she sat silent, her unyielding eye stabbing at the fear and rebellion that contested within Lion Hunter. At length, she spoke again, her words brittle with purpose.

"Know this also, young Lion Hunter—I shall make a fierce warrior of you, a warrior great beyond your boy-dreams. My kindness to Crow Woman is my promise to you." Then, abruptly, "We break camp, now."

At her direction, Lion Hunter broke down the medicine woman's lodge, packed the horses and, mounted on his father's black gelding, silently rode away from the abandoned Wolf Ridge village site and his stolen life. His legs hugged the animal's huge chest as he leaned into its neck, absorbing its warmth and familiar feel.

He rode silently, behind his fearsome new mentor and her husband, Ghost Head, who, after breaking his own camp, hailed the two to follow. The three rode at the rear of the village caravan, which was the old holy man's preference.

Muffled sounds drifted back eerily through the murk of night—horse hooves clopping, whispered conversations, and the scrape of travois' pulled behind ponies over uneven earth—each an unnerving reminder of the sinister reasons for their night travel, and, Lion Hunter's dread of what was to come.

2

Ponies, finally shed of their shaggy winter coats, grazed languidly in the nearby pasture and idleness settled over the Wolf Ridge village. The approach of summer, foretold by the first truly warm days of the advancing season, was upon them. Young fillies and colts, grown out of their newborn awkwardness, were now playfully testing recently learned skills upon one another.

It was three months since Lion Hunter came to stay with Kills-In-The-Dark, to be taught, by her, the ways of the warrior. Other young braves trained for warrior-hood with real warriors, men, so he remained embarrassed that a woman was his mentor. However, he lacked any alternative and was obliged to swallow his pride and follow her instructions.

She is ugly, and her disrespect for others is harsh. The Spirit Fathers must surely wish her a forever-life so they do not have to live near to her when it is her time to move to the spirit world.

He stood away from her lodge, looking at his mentor through the teepee's open flap as she busied herself tying bound strands of herbs to the teepee's interior framework. Unlike other women of the band, she clothed herself, as did Lion Hunter, in the traditional breechcloth and full-length leggings of Wolf Ridge warriors. At this moment, her torso, also like that of a warrior, was bare. The two of them had returned from collecting buffalo dung for the night's fire and she, upon entering the lodge, had removed the rough, black-dyed buckskin shirt she wore during their outing. Hard muscle corded her solid torso and arms as she stood on tiptoes stretching overhead.

Lion Hunter found himself looking at her breasts. Both nipples had been brutally carved away—a punishing practice amongst the women of certain tribes assuring slave women taken by their men could not successfully nurse infants. As with the hideous scarring on her face, she bore these cruel reminders of her time among the Blackfeet with seeming indifference.

Lion Hunter reluctantly came to admire her toughness. He accepted her use of male weapons, especially with the bow and even the lance, which was more skillful than his—perhaps even equal to his father's. Nothing from his past, though, prepared him for this woman who was now his teacher, whose lodge he was forced to join as an unwelcome guest.

Woman, why are you so strange, so unlike all others of our band?

There was one thing Lion Hunter did understand about his mentor, a thing of greater fascination to him than either toughness or skill in the use of male weapons. Kills-In-The-Dark was cunning. Not just sly, but truly calculating in the way she manipulated those around her. Not ugly manipulation for, despite the general insolence that was her way, as a whole the things she did seemed less often to benefit herself than they did others. For many of these things, her shaman husband, Ghost Head, was her voice. In recent times, Lion Hunter often heard her influence in important decisions spoken of by Camp Chief Weasel Bear and others.

They do not notice her sway because their hearts have only dread for her mutilated face and body—that and her strangeness.

Unlike her, his parents had been straightforward in their dealings with those who lived around them, close friends with some, neighbors to others, and more distant to those few remaining. Kills-In-The-Dark walked among the people of their village like a shadow, an unsettling spirit of mysterious purpose. Lion Hunter, who now secretly studied her at every turn, came to respect the raw effectiveness of her shrewd side.

As respect for his teacher grew so did a concern that others, blinded to her skills and cleverness by such dreadful appearance and odd behavior, might view him as weak for being in her charge. His reputation among the other young braves as a discarded orphan troubled him. Also, he had noticed soft-eyed and curious glances cast in his direction by a young girl named Willow. Her family's standing in the village was lowly, but Lion Hunter enjoyed the unfamiliar feelings caused by her peeks and he did not wish them to end.

Aye, sweet Willow, how do you make my heart sing with these peeks?

Lion Hunter had neither lodge nor family to offer as standing among his people. He had only this abnormal relationship with a strange medicine woman, and he had not even been on his vision quest yet. No matter his heart's urgings, he was not yet ready for a true relationship with any girl.

I have no joy to give to you, Willow. But I will work my hardest to become a warrior, to be thought of as worthy. Until then, I will do what this strange teacher tells me to do, and I will hope for good things.

In fact, Kills-In-The-Dark asked little of him in the way of camp chores, requiring only that he accompany her wherever she went—not as an escort but as a student. She demanded that he understand both how and why she did the things she did. She called this way of understanding a "think-habit." Among the many things he learned was where various herbs could be found, but no teaching by her was to be quite so simple as that. She demanded that he understand why each herb was to be found at its favored location, and beyond that, how knowing these things might be important to his and his people's future.

He was proud of the progress he made with her think-habit and proud the events of his life had begun threading themselves together like the carefully woven web of a spider. Frustration came less often now as he focused on the importance of learning to become a warrior rather than simply wanting to be one. His confidence began to soar with the belief that acquiring knowledge and understanding was now within his grasp. He was becoming a man.

Her harsh voice startled him out of reflection. "Why do you stare at me, Boy?"

He lifted his eyes from her mutilated breasts to find her glowering at him from within the lodge. He willed his blush to be gone as he deflected her question by asking, "Why do you wear the clothes of a warrior?"

She scowled back at him. "Do you mock me?" Annoyance tinged her words.

"No," he retreated, without moving physically. He stared back at her—jaw thrust forward, in silent defiance of the moment's potential for retribution.

Kills-In-The-Dark continued staring at him for the space of several breaths. Finally, a smirk chased the annoyance from her expression. Then, standing up straight, she cupped both mutilated breasts in her hands and shook them at him.

"They are broken," she mocked. "Do you stare with the pride of a warrior or the need of a puppy?" Not waiting for a response she abruptly turned her back and returned to her task.

Lion Hunter briefly pondered what had just taken place and smiled, proud he had used the think-habit throughout the conversation.

Who is the student now, Broken Tits?

Kills-In-The-Dark, her back to him, concealed her own smile.

* * *

Lion Hunter and his mentor walked silently, both enjoying the warmth of the day. They were returning from a hunt. Four rabbits, freshly gutted and stowed in the game pouch hanging from his shoulder, spoke to their success. A curious thought popped into Lion Hunter's consciousness and immediately began agitating for understanding.

"Aunt," he began, addressing Kills-In-The-Dark respectfully, "when I was young and first tried to make a deer kill, my deer would always know I stalked her and quickly run away. So father taught me to find the path she walked upon to reach her feed place each day. In that way I was to know where she would be the next day, and when. He said I should lie down on the side of the path during the darkness to make ready for my kill. Then, in the morning light, if I had been very still, he said, the deer would walk up and sniff me but would not understand that I was there to take her life. He said she would step over me with no fear in her heart and no understanding of my purpose, and could then easily be taken. I understand now the truth of this hunting way, but I do not know why it is so."

"Boy, how do you think the deer knows when she is hunted?"

He pondered the question. "When she sees the hunter?"

"Does she not see you when you lie near her feed path?"

"Yes… she sees me," he answered thoughtfully. "She is cautious, but she sees me."

"What thing is different between your stalking and your lay-down that she flees from one but not the other?"

"I move for only one small breath in the lay-down, when I kill her with my arrow after she has passed. Is it that I move so fast she does not have time to run?"

"When she is feeding at the edge of the meadow and you ride by upon your pony, she has much time to flee, yet she does not." His mentor cocked her head to the side as she waited for his response.

"Well, if I stop to look at her while on my pony, or if I move toward her, she flees then." Lion Hunter hedged.

"And do you look at her when you lie quiet near her feed path?"

"No. Father said I must never look in her eyes."

"What thing is in your heart when you are laying still and not looking at this deer who comes to you sniffing?"

"My heart reminds me that I must lay very still and not look at her if I am to make my kill."

"She sees what you do but not what is in your heart?"

Lion Hunter scoffed. "I know she cannot see what is in my heart."

"What does she see in your stalking that tells her your heart's thoughts—this thing that she cannot see in your lay-down? When you answer that, you will know why she runs from your stalking."

With that final statement, Kills-In-The-Dark turned and walked away, leaving Lion Hunter behind. He stood pondering her final statement with no doubt that the answer to his question was buried in the words of their conversation. He also knew she would not speak to him further on the matter.

How can a deer's eyes be so easily fooled by a hunter lying on the ground?

He shook his head and continued on toward their campsite. He resolved to think on the matter while skinning the rabbits, but the question's answer continued to elude him.

***

The conflict with custom posed by Lion Hunter's unusual relationship with Kills-In-The-Dark caused an undercurrent of puzzlement among many of the adult members of the band. There was also his newly acquired swagger, not yet wholly derived from competence, but swagger still. Lion Hunter had, at last, begun to feel as though his life was significant.

Then, a woman from their people's Sheep Eater clan came to visit her sister—War Chief Crow Chaser's wife. The woman was searching for a husband. That search, and a war chief named Carries His Lion, were about to dramatically impact Lion Hunter's life.

3

"Carries-His-Lion is foolish, but he is healthy, and he is War Chief of the Lion Shadows." Sees-The-Sky forced her contention, knowing mention of the upstart Lion Shadow warrior society would upset her husband—a chief of the much older, more highly respected, Badger warrior society.

"He would make a good husband to my sister," she pressed, squinting her ill-tempered will across the lodge fire pit at her husband, Crow Chaser. "He is a fit hunter."

"Carries-His-Lion is foolish," Crow Chaser responded, his tone, if not his words, resolutely neutral. He picked up a piece of kindling and jabbed at the fire pit's cold ashes.

"My sister crowds my lodge," his wife continued.

Crow Chaser flinched in response to the words.

Is this lodge no longer mine? Must all things bow to your bitter will, old woman? Even the customs of our people?

"I tire of her endless complaints," Sees-The-Sky went on. "My family sends her here to find a husband, but she is too lazy to be a wife. I think maybe they just sent her here."

"Your sister is lazy, Sky." Still stung by his wife's reference to "her lodge," he exhaled loudly, shifting to look out the open entrance flap. The distant horizon and its dark line of mountains tempted his growing sense of rebellion.

"I think you should go to him. Make him see the importance of taking a good wife," Sees-The-Sky pressed.

"He is too stupid," Crow Chaser groused. But there was little hope in his tone.

He is arrogant and knows no respect. He understands only the dishonor of public ridicule.

"Your head is soft, old man. Do you like her snoring in your lodge, so loud no one else can sleep? And her eating, always like a starving grizzly?"

So, when it suits you, the lodge belongs to me.

"Humph!" Crow Chaser answered. The eloquent nuance of his favored response to vexing issues emphasized the depth of his displeasure at being drawn into this taxing discussion. Unwittingly, his hand combed through his long hair, finding and fingering the long scar that made an angry red surge down out of his hairline, and through a mangled ear.

I am the only remaining War Chief of the Badger warrior society, old woman. Is it too much to honor my lodge by not calling it yours?

In the end, his wife would have her way or he would have no peace. He closed his eyes, waiting for what he knew came next.

"Go, then. Why do you remain? My sister will return soon enough. Return to curse my lodge with her worthless ways." Sky stood, and glared down at him.

He looked up meaning to lock eyes with her, but momentary resolve was no match for the ambush lurking in her squint-eyed glare. The old chief rose, struck with a sudden wistfulness for the exhilarating danger of faraway physical combat.

He stood and massaged his back, one last rebellion against her harrying.

She smiled, handing him his dress shirt as he exited. Smiles were infrequent visitors to her face, but they were the closest things to marital reward sharing his lodge with her had produced for him over the last several years. He grunted a long-suffering "thanks"—for the shirt. He pulled it down over his head and set off on his assigned mission.

"Ho, Lion, it is I, Crow Chaser. I would speak to you."

"What do you want?" came a gruff response from within the younger War Chief's lodge.

"To speak. As I have said."

Is it not enough that I have come begging at the entrance to your lodge, you arrogant skunk's ass?

"Come, then." A groaning exhale came from within—louder than the invitation had been.

"Sit," the young chief muttered upon Crow Chaser's entrance. His unenthusiastic invitation was accompanied by a hand gesture indicating the honorary position for guests near the lodge fire pit at the teepee's center.

The two War Chiefs sat cross-legged opposite one another. The impatient twenty-six-year-old, whose thick body sat rigid as he stared across the fire at Crow Chaser, was obviously irritated by the necessity of showing the old chief the respect of admission to his lodge.

Crow Chaser looked at the four parallel ridges of ugly scar tissue that raked from Carries-His-Lion's right shoulder, down over most of his upper arm. A flashy wound left by the War Chief's namesake. Crow Chaser's fingers again crept up and touched his own scar.

"Carries-His-Lion, I would have a smoke with you, and speak of marriage."

"What?" the young chief erupted. "Do you mock me, Crow Chaser?"

Crow Chaser, his dark eyes and long face expressionless, went stiff inside.

Do I mock you? Do I mock you! You are an arrogant, stupid dung beetle. Of course I mock you.

"I do not. My wife's sister will make a fine wife for some prosperous warrior."

Carries-His-Lion looked at Crow Chaser, his wide face and eyes stricken with disbelief.

"Your wife's sister is lazy! Camp wives find many unkind things to say about her. Besides," he added, "I think she is maybe a chin-wag-wife to any husband."

Crow Chaser caught the not-so-subtle allusion to his own wife's notoriously disagreeable whispering campaigns.

"Are so many women crowding your teepee's entrance then?"

Carries-His-Lion stood abruptly, the cords in his powerfully muscled neck standing out as he glared down at his unwelcome visitor. "No smoke," he snarled, yanking back the lodge's entrance flap and gesturing with his chin. "I would have you leave my lodge. Now!"

Crow Chaser exited in a huff, his wife's mission failed. Worse, he had to return to his own lodge and face the raging anger the young chieftain's response would bring from her.

Carries-His-Lion's ill-mannered rejection of Sees-The-Sky's plan landed on Crow Chaser's lodge with the force of the black whirling winds that carry all things away. The old chief fled his lodge the moment his raging wife turned her back, knowing, but not caring, that far worse would follow the discovery of his absence.

Crow Chaser was on a desperate mission to find a hunting companion—any hunting companion. He knew he would pay later for his untimely 'disappearance,' but he could stomach no more women problems, and he didn't want to be around for the worst of her anger. By midafternoon, both he and a sympathetic friend slipped out of camp on an otter hunt expected to last a week.

* * *

When Prairie Gale, the camp wailer, raced up to Sees-The-Sky's lodge she was near bursting with news. Winded, she hailed her friend between deep gasps for air.

"Sky," she screamed, her shrill voice shredding the surrounding air. "Carries-His-Lion … he makes disrespect to your sister … among his … Lion Shadow warriors."

Sees-The-Sky poked her head out of the lodge entrance, staring up at her chunky friend through slit eyes. Prairie Gale, though now standing upright, was still noisily recovering from her run. Having delivered her news, the young woman spread her arms and self-consciously shrugged—a serpentine dance along the unusually decorative fringe of her shirt emphasized the gesture.

"How do you know this thing?" Sees-The-Sky demanded, feeling the muscles of her face cinch down into a comfortable scowl.

"Makes-Snake-Run told me. It is from her husband. She says Carries-His-Lion calls your sister a fat chin-wag and laughs that Crow Chaser came begging for a husband to take her away from his own lodge."

* * *

Sees-The-Sky, her sagging jowls quivering with anger, immediately began to plot retaliation for Carries-His-Lion's arrogant rejection of her will. Hush-hush conversations with the women of surrounding lodges produced sniggering agreement—the self-important Carries-His-Lion had exceeded the limits of camp etiquette. His current act of insolence was only one in a flood of many, but this insult had fallen upon the wrong woman. Vengeance was owed, and now all that remained was the arrival of nightfall.

* * *

Darkness settled over the camp. A wet chill funneled out of Beaver Creek's tree-lined channel, gathering in the surrounding lowlands where the band had set up their village camp.

Lion Hunter, huddled in the lean-to he had erected near his mentor's teepee, pulled his rabbit-fur over his shoulders. The soothing warmth from his small fire flickered over his bare chest, ebbing and flowing with the night's breeze. He was fletching an arrow.

After binding the ends of split feather quill to an arrow shaft with chewed sinew, he began applying hide glue to the gap between quill and shaft. He was pressing it into place when the end of his blanket fell forward.

He caught the blanket with his elbow, awkwardly cinching it back with his other forearm to keep the fur's silky smoothness from becoming fouled.

Pleased that he saved the blanket, Lion Hunter shifted his concentration to re-positioning the arrow in his lap and to pressing quill and shaft together to make them stick.

"Come. Now!" It was Kills-In-The-Dark.

Her exit from the teepee and abrupt words so surprised Lion Hunter that he dropped the gooey stick he had applied the glue with, and it fell against his legging before dropping into the dirt.

Kills-In-The-Dark swept by him and was already striding rapidly off through the camp.

Flinging the arrow shaft to the dirt, he lurched to his feet, scowling at her retreating back. Unaware and uncaring, she continued on.

Lion Hunter glowered down at the fouled black-dyed legging he made and wore so proudly. After suitable delay, he pulled his blanket closer, and, his thoughts surly, set off after the medicine woman. Upon overtaking her, he fell into step at her shoulder rather than following along behind, as was his custom.

They passed Camp Chief Weasel Bear's lodge, and Lion Hunter saw its entrance flap swish aside. He heard the whispering sounds of clothing moving as someone exited. Glancing sideways, he caught the camp chief just coming to an upright position. Weasel Bear nodded a silent greeting to him before stepping aside for his wife to exit.

Lion Hunter wondered at the two leaving their lodge so late. He hadn't heard the sounds of dance or any other crowd-attracting event since he and his mentor began their hasty walk—a walk now taking them toward the far side of the camp. He glanced about, just darkness and cone-shaped teepees, the tips of the supporting lodge poles jutting finger-like into the moonlit sky. Many pale shadows silently drifted by while he and his mentor padded on. Just as he determined to ask where they were going, she stopped.

Lion Hunter glanced about again, immediately picking out two dark figures sitting on the ground nearby. Mere silhouettes, they were shaded from the moonlight by the nearest cone lodge. The woman giggled softly, leaning close to her companion as he whispered into her ear. Lion Hunter sifted through the surrounding night shadows with his peripheral vision, picking out several additional dark figures not previously noticed, each lingering in moon-shadowed obscurity near this or that teepee.

Hearing soft footsteps from behind, he turned. Weasel Bear and his wife walked up to the whispering couple and sat down with them. The four began murmuring amongst themselves.

All of the surrounding shadow-persons, both seated and standing, were facing the same teepee. That teepee was the one directly before where he and his mentor now stood. It was the lodge of longtime bully to Lion Hunter, War Chief Carries-His-Lion.

Lion Hunter's breathing quickened. He had no idea what event had been planned here, or what might be about to happen to the obnoxious War Chief of the Lion Shadows, who openly called him Crow Bastard, but he sensed and hoped that it would be unpleasant. He was certain he would enjoy whatever was to come.

Unlike other villagers nearby, Kills-In-The-Dark had stopped in the open. Lion Hunter, standing beside her, noted that the rising moon would light their positions before all others if the War Chief were to exit his lodge.

Kills-In-The-Dark lowered herself to the ground sitting cross-legged. When Lion Hunter continued to stand, she tugged at his leggings and nodded toward a spot next to her. While she turned to face the teepee's entrance, Lion Hunter sat, feeling giddy anticipation. He noticed the big warrior's camp pony had been mischievously untied from its picket.

He turned his head to stare at the moonlit canyons of scar tissue shadowing Kills-In-The-Dark's face. Pride swelled up in him.

I am probably the only one in our band who has the courage to look directly at her face.

She and I are one.

She turned to him, her voice a whisper for the first time in his memory.

"Remember, if a warrior is to speak to you in anger it must be through me. I am your mentor. You will be silent. You are not yet a warrior, but you must … be strong like the great warriors of your family who have gone on, to be with their Spirit Fathers."

She speaks of my father and uncle. She has not done this before.

Lion Hunter nodded, chin lifted, heart pounding in his ears. He straightened his back and faced the teepee before him.

The first ghost-like voice materialized from the surrounding darkness, clearly disguised by its owner.

"What is this stink?" it demanded loudly.

Silence.

"It is the stink of a lion cub shitting herself with fear, I think," a disembodied answer responded from the opposite direction. Soft giggling emerged, spirit-like, from the surrounding moon-shadowed darkness. They were ridiculing Carries-His-Lion's name taking—his fight with an attacking she-lion. Lion Hunter reflected back on the scrawny scar-faced lion he had slain and laid at the big warrior's teepee entrance two years before—the very lion the big warrior claimed years before to have bravely pulled from his pony's back and knifed in a ferocious melee.

A third disguised voice bellowed, "What thing does a brave warrior do with a helpless female… l-i-i-i-on?" The question ended with a sudden high-pitched squeal.

Several snickers followed, again from the surrounding shadows. Lion Hunter found himself grinning widely, enjoying the scandalous mockery being heaped upon his antagonist.

"Something harmless for a warrior to stick his tail into when no woman will have him." Giggles followed from multiple locations.

There was abrupt movement from within the teepee.

"Tail?" laughed the first. "His pee dribbles down his leg because he can find no tail to pull out." Open laughter pealed from the shadowed area where Camp Chief Weasel Bear sat.

"Is that why no woman will have him?" a new voice chuckled. "No wonder he has so many winters and not yet married."

Angry epithets now came from inside the dark lodge. Hasty movements jostled against the insides of the teepee's thick leather hides. Lion Hunter grinned.

Ha! So, Carries-His-Kitten, how does contempt taste when it is yours to eat?

"What, no pleasure tool? Can there be joy for any woman with one like him? Does he take in a lion's shadow to keep him warm at night?"

Loud kissing sounds from several directions pierced the night, followed by rapid slapping sounds, skin on skin, then louder hoots from the surrounding darkness. Lion Hunter laughed as well but immediately stopped when he felt his mentor's jab to his ribs and sensed her piercing stare.

The outraged warrior burst from his teepee, fury contorting his face.

"Who shames me? Say these words to my face," he bellowed still fumbling with the knot of his breechcloth. Silence charged with restrained energy engulfed the surrounding blackness.

The big War Chief's glare quickly found Lion Hunter and his mentor but instantly darted away when more kissing sounds sprang up from behind his teepee. Carries-His-Lion spun and crashed headlong into his loosened lodge pony, sending the animal racing off into the night. The warrior quickly recovered and resumed his pursuit of the latest attack upon his manhood. The loud skin slapping resumed, this time from the shadows near the front of his lodge. The furious man spun around again. He rushed back but again found only silence.

He stopped, breathing hard before Lion Hunter and Kills-In-The-Dark. His eyes flashed about the surrounding shadows, then jerked back to the seated medicine woman and her grinning apprentice.

"Why do you sit before my teepee, witch woman?" he barked.

Kills-In-The-Dark did not answer the big warrior's demanding question. Instead, she stared back at him with silent hostility. An eerie silence fell over all who were nearby. Lion Hunter, wallowing in mirth moments before, suddenly felt a chilling sense of imminent danger.

"I speak to you, scar face. Do you not hear me?" Carries-His-Lion roared, hunching forward, his hand on the hilt of his knife.

She returned his stare in continued silence.

Again, his eyes flashed around the perimeter of shadows, not fixing until they came back to Lion Hunter. The warrior's shadowed facial expression slowly relaxed. With a deep breath, he stood up to his full height and squared his thick shoulders.

"I see you have brought your Crow bastard," he said to the medicine woman, staring down into Lion Hunter's eyes.

Lion Hunter leaped to his feet, his jaw quivering with anger as he glared back at the angry War Chief. After a moment of silence, Kills-In-The-Dark lightly touched her young apprentice's ankle. From the corner of his eye, Lion Hunter saw her looking up at him. For long moments, he continued to stare into the smirking bully's eyes. Finally, he sat, fixing his eyes on the ground before him, breathing deeply and willing his fury to recede.

"Lion Hunter is not yet a warrior…but I am." Her flinty declaration knifed through the eerie silence surrounding the trio. Lion Hunter, suddenly fearful of what was about to happen, looked from the angry warrior to his mentor then back.

The man's eyes slowly moved from Lion Hunter and locked once again onto the seated medicine woman. A long moment later, he laughed dismissively.

"Be careful, Witch. Do not tempt the end of your ugly life. I will not be mocked by a woman," he said, stepping back and sticking out his chin.

"So the mysterious night voices tell us all. I have no part of this scolding tonight. I came only to listen to the words others gift to you. To listen . . . and to watch."

"Leave now, before I smash your pet bastard into the ground." He seemed to have given up the idea of threatending Kills-In-The-Dark, but his voice still held a bitter threat, this time for Lion Hunter.

"I would defend him." Her words were stone hard, her intense single-eyed stare piercing.

"I think I might cut your throat, ugly slave woman who calls herself a warrior." The thick-limbed warrior renewed his threats to Lion Hunter's mentor, muscles again taut as he glowered down at her.

"Not four moons past our people banished one who murdered another of his own people. I think if banished, you would not survive the wilderness alone. Not only are there no others to swagger before, I think the bears maybe, or a real lion, would not be so impressed by your loud boasts."

Carries-His-Lion's eyes swiveled away from hers, searching the surrounding crowd of shadows. This time he appeared less angry than he did concerned, about the many eyes watching and the notion of banishment. After a brief pause, he eased himself into a less threatening position then stepped back from the confrontation.

At that moment Kills-In-The-Dark came to a full standing position before him.

"I was slave to five Blackfeet, that is true," she growled. "They were two wives and three warriors. And the things they did to me made me look as I do this night, but you must know their five heads now hang above my lodge fire, as they will forever."

More silence.

The angry warrior stood rigid, chin jutting.

"Carries-His-Lion," she hissed, "the coyote spirit did not collect these trophies for me. I did that myself." She paused. "I am a warrior, but I do not play at coup-counting like you and your brother campfire warriors.

"Those who take pain to make themselves my enemies die by my hand. Their spirits die with them for I speak their names out loudly each day so the Spirit Fathers will believe them still alive and not allow them to cross to the spirit world beyond."

She maintained eye contact a moment longer before Carries-His-Lion, giving off a loud, "harrumph," spun on his heel and abruptly reentered his teepee. A few more half-hearted kissing sounds went unheeded.

Kills-In-The-Dark turned to Lion Hunter and motioned him to follow as she began walking back toward her lodge. Lion Hunter climbed to his feet and trailed along, this time proudly walking behind his mentor.

* * *

Kills-In-The-Dark, freshly returned from a visit to her husband's teepee, walked up to Lion Hunter and squatted down on her haunches beside him. Silent, she watched as he repeatedly worked a willow stem back and forth through a narrow-grooved rock, shaving it into the straight form of an arrow shaft.

"So, Hunter, tell me," she said after a long silence, "what did you understand of Carries-His-Lion, last night?"

Lion Hunter, eager to talk about the incident, had forced himself to wait for her to bring up the subject.

"I saw you go to a place where Carries-His-Lion would see you before all others. I saw you sit down. I saw you help him remember about banishment then wait until worry chased away his bravery before you stood to face him. Then I saw you make a warning."

Lion Hunter had been thinking and rethinking the incident since first returning to his lean-to the night before.

"And what of these things?"

"I think he angers easily and is then dangerous."

"Do you think he fears me?"

"No… I think maybe not. I think he fears banishment and that maybe his spirit will not make its journey to the spirit world if he is made to leave his people."

"So why did I do these things and why did I take you with me?"

Lion Hunter considered these new questions. He was still thinking through the meanings of this part of the incident and didn't want to respond yet. When she continued her silent eye contact, he yielded.

"I think maybe to protect me, but maybe he hates me even more now. I wish more time to think on these questions."

She looked at him for a long moment and then asked, "When you stood before him, did you need to look up to see his eyes?"

Lion Hunter blinked, surprised by the revelation her question prompted.

I did not!

"No." The response leaked from his lips, more question than answer.

"Did your mother ever tell you your true father was a Crow warrior?"

"No," he said, the word barely audible. He waited, his hand now clinching the medicine bag hanging from his neck.

"Your mother was tall and pretty."

Lion Hunter winced at the word 'was.' He did not yet wish to think of his mother as dead. But what Kills-In-The-Dark said about his mother's height and attractiveness was true.

"The Crow people are tall and pretty. Do your eyes not see the truth of our Wolf Ridge people? We are shorter, and thicker, and have heavy round faces."

Lion Hunter stood waiting, gripped by the corroboration of his heritage.

"Hunter, you are already taller than Carries-His-Lion. Did you see that when you stood before him?"

Lion Hunter, the fifteen-and-a-half-year-old, nodded his head slowly.

"I think maybe you will be a pretty warrior someday, Hunter. Yes?" With that question, her scarred face contorted into a smile.

4

Most in the village expected that shaming the arrogant young chief of the Shadow warriors would modify his strong-willed behavior enough so life in the camp could return to the relaxed hum of daily routines. But that is not what happened.

Carries-His-Lion had no concern for the expectations of others. The hotheaded young chief was too full of himself to accept public ridicule without retaliation. He was both a War Chief and the leader of a warrior society—the same warrior society currently awarded the honor of serving as the band's camp police. His mind was full of anger and vengeance, and he had all the power he needed to retaliate for the dishonor of being publicly ridiculed.

Early the following morning, two Shadow warriors approached a badger warrior's lodge and stood outside loudly demanding the dung dropped overnight by his picketed lodge pony be cleaned up immediately. The problem was, they picked Fish's lodge to police. He was not just a Badger warrior—he was nephew to Crow Chaser, husband of the ill-tempered woman who organized the shaming. From the beginning, there was no mistaking the true purpose of the two Shadow warriors' complaint, and the entire camp quickly turned out to witness the loud commotion that followed.

Fish, like his uncle Crow Chaser, was a proud Badger warrior, not a Lion Shadow warrior, and he responded to the camp police demands by charging out of his lodge to challenge the notion that Shadow warriors were even real warriors, much less qualified to police the conduct of Badger warriors.

Others from both warrior societies responded, and the incident quickly escalated into a shoving match fraught with danger to the village peace. Only the intervention of several camp wives, Fish's wife among them, prevented an escalation to more serious conflict between the angry knots of men.

"Look, I am cleaning up the dung!" Fish's wife shouted at them while scooping up the clumps of waste and dropping them into the folded lap of her dress. "Why do you fight like children?" Her voice cracking, she clamped her mouth shut and stared at the men.

All the wives, moments before yanking at the tussling warriors, gathered around her in support.

Still bristling, the warriors stood silent, glaring at one another—two factions teetering on the edge of violence.

"All ponies make dung," Camp Chief Weasel Bear's wife announced, stepping forward from among the gathered wives. "Maybe no ponies should be picketed in the camp so there will be less flies and more peace," she continued, her eyebrows arched in challenging suggestion as she looked from one warrior to the next.

"Yes," a second woman agreed, then another, and yet another until all were nodding their heads while eyeing their respective husbands meaningfully.

The united position of the wives challenged the most prominent of all warrior privileges—his finest war pony proudly picketed at his lodge entrance. Other ponies were pastured, not allowed in camp. One by one the warriors stepped away from their hostilities and an uneasy peace grudgingly settled over the immediate incident.

* * *

The two Shadow warriors who started the fracas, however, now found themselves without the victory they had set out to achieve. It was no surprise when the same two pompously turned their inspections to the rest of the camp. Strutting about, they denounced the placing of meat drying racks and various other "woman" items left outside certain teepees—those linked to the wives suspected of being involved in the previous night's scolding.

Carries-His-Lion began his own retaliatory conduct—verbal attacks on others, bouts of brash threats and menacing glares, all over the previous night's scolding. By late afternoon, the band's women, led by the camp chief's wife, demanded loudly that a council be convened and action taken to defuse the camp's growing tension.

"Carries-His-Lion is head of the camp police," they argued loudly, "how can we feel safe when he stomps around so always-angry?"

By that afternoon, the Lion Shadow chief's conduct had become so outrageous that only the two Lion Shadows who instigated the morning's hostilities with their targeted camp inspection now continued to defend him. Still, Carries-His-Lion's fury grew.

Patience exhausted and the afternoon's temperature continuing to rise, Weasel Bear called for an emergency council-smoke. It was to take place at dusk.

As darkness approached, the band's five current chiefs, including Carries-His-Lion, gathered in Weasel Bear's lodge. Pony Man, the band's respected storyteller, was also there as was Ghost Head, the old holy man. The inclusion of both the frail storyteller and Ghost Head was unusual, but they were there at Weasel Bear's request and none among the regular council members objected.

The group seated themselves around Weasel Bear's lodge fire. While Carries-His-Lion fumed silently, the rest gazed down into its smoldering coals waiting until the camp chief's wife unpacked his ceremonial pipe-bundle and presented it to him.

Though this particular council threatened to be fierier than most, councils among the Wolf Ridge people were always treated as festive occasions by the rest of the camp and this one was no exception. Councils were public events, gatherings of the band's most respected members, a collective decision-making process that the entire village turned out for.

Many children gathered around Weasel-Bear's teepee. Several boys lay on the ground, their heads poking beneath the teepee's hide flaps eagerly waiting for important news they could report to the less brazen who waited behind them. Other children tussled and tripped over one another kicking up dust and enjoying the collective gathering. Camp women huddled here and there, speaking in conspiratorial tones about what things might be done if the situation was not satisfactorily resolved and peace quickly restored. Separate from the other onlookers were Carries-His-Lion's two Shadow warrior conspirators, their arms folded across their chests as they stood in sullen support of their leader.

Sees-The-Sky, the ill-tempered instigator of the previous night's shaming, lurked near Fish's thirteen-year-old son, whose head was one of those poked beneath the dusty flap of buffalo skin at the bottom of Weasel Bear's teepee. The old woman impatiently nudged his thigh with her toe, awaiting a report on the council's proceedings.

Weasel Bear, his heavily creased face set with sternness befitting his position as Camp Chief, began by nodding to each council member and waiting for return nods until each had acknowledged the smoke-council's opening. He carefully removed the soft-stone pipe bowl and its stem from the bundled elk skin and fitted the two together. After tamping the bowl with a mixture of tobacco and willow bark, he gathered a small ember from the fire with a forked twig and dropped it into the bowl. When the tobacco lit, he dumped the ember and drew heavily at the pipe's stem. He held in the smoke for a long moment then exhaled, fanning the white cloud so its billowing haze found each of those who sat around the fire pit. He completed his part of the opening ceremony by solemnly presenting the pipe to the four corners of his people's world, then to the spirit world above, and finally to sacred Mother Earth below murmuring a prayer for each.

Next, he passed his people's most potent totem to Crow Chaser who, in accordance with his camp standing, sat on Weasel Bear's left. Crow Chaser repeated the opening ritual and, grunting his accustomed, "humph," passed the pipe to the council member on his left.

The pipe made its way around the circle, with each of the first four chiefs, in turn, reverently performing the same ritual. The fifth, however, was Carries-His-Lion, still angry and visibly impatient for the moment of his turn to speak.

The young chief impetuously snatched the pipe from Beaver Tail—the chief seated on his right—and, clamping the pipe's stem between his teeth, jerked in a quick breath then expelled the smoke in a furious gust. He omitted the sacred offerings and abruptly thrust the pipe out to his left without even looking at Ghost Head, the next in the circle.

Carries-His-Lion glared around the circle making eye contact with each chief, one after the other. Solemn-faced, each looked back at him and nodded as the pipe ceremony continued.

Ghost Head, eyes closed, bowed and murmured a prayer before completing his ceremonial draw. He then handed the talisman to Pony Man, who sat last in the council circle.

"I am honored you have invited me to sit among you," Pony Man said, acknowledging each of the others in the circle with a nod.

Upon completing his offering, Pony Man handed the pipe back to Weasel Bear.

In silence, the camp chief methodically tapped out the last of the bowl's ashes before carefully disassembling its pieces and rewrapping them. He handed the bundle to his waiting wife and turned his eyes back to the fire.

Carries-His-Lion waited, tension playing at the muscles in his jaw as Weasel Bear's silence dragged on.

By custom, Weasel Bear led council discussions, followed by the next in rank, and so on, just as with the pipe.

Finally, still looking into the flames at his feet, Weasel Bear spoke, his tone grave.

"The warmth of summer comes to us early this year."

Lion squirmed and gritted his teeth while each of the others nodded in solemn agreement.

After another long pause Crow Chaser, the next in rank, delivered his input.

"Humph!"

The old Badger chief, who dependably sat his position at council, rarely used the opportunity to make more complete commentary. But he did use this occasion to openly glare at Carries-His-Lion, whose behavior and the resulting camp disturbance the council had gathered to deal with.

Carries-His-Lion responded immediately, thrusting his jaw forward and opening his mouth as though to blurt out a response to the older chief's silent disrespect, but every head in the circle suddenly jerked up in preemptive rebuke, and he strangled off the intended retort. Barely able to restrain himself, he swallowed hard, and dug his fingers into the earth at his sides.

There followed another lengthy silence before Many Dogs, the next in order, shifted his gimpy right leg to a more comfortable position then spoke.

"What you say is true, Weasel Bear. The ponies have shed their winter coats early. They know, I think, that the warm moons will stay with us."

All in the circle again nodded their agreement, that is, all except Carries-His-Lion who sat ridged, jaw muscles now trembling.

Beaver Tail spoke next. Only slightly older than Carries-His-Lion, the smiling young chief sat just before him in the circle.

"The camp dogs, too, have shed their winter coats—except for Fish's ugly three-legger who is too proud to show his stump."

All but Lion chuckled and nodded in response to his droll quip about Crow Chaser's nephew's dog.

Sensing his turn, Lion opened his mouth to speak but was abruptly cut off by Beaver Tail, who unexpectedly resumed speaking.

"Those of my lodge do not sleep with buffalo robes for two moons now," he added.

Mouth snapped shut, and lips pinched tight, Carries-His-Lion seethed. This time he waited, teeth grinding. At the very moment he again decided his turn had come, Beaver Tail began speaking, again.

"Yes, summer comes early, I think." At the conclusion of these words Beaver Tail smirked at Carries-His-Lion then turned his attention back to the fire, as had the others.

Finally, it was Carries-His-Lion's turn.

"Why do we speak of warmth? What care is the summer to us here?" he exploded. "So many in the village plot treachery. They mock order. For what do we have camp police?"

So furious was his outburst, spittle spewed on the coals before him, sizzling in exclamation of his tumbling words.

The group's imperturbable silence continued.

"What craziness is this talk?" Carries-His-Lion bell-owed, striking himself violently in the forehead with the heel of his hand as though attempting to knock away some murky obstruction to understanding. His eyes whipped around the group unsuccessfully trying to lock with any one of them. Failing, he lifted his hands overhead, "What madness is this?" he demanded of the smoke-stained vent flap at the top of the teepee.

Immediately left of the outraged warrior, Ghost Head, the old holy man, sat gazing down into the fire's embers, his gnarled hands resting calmly on his knees. Eyes still downcast, he mumbled a few words to himself then raised his voice, both tone and words settling gently over the pall Carries-His-Lion's outburst left behind.

"The summer's warm breezes come upon us like tender new grasses, showing hope that the real world will welcome their arrival—that the hearts of we real men will fill with noble thoughts of preparation for their time, even as our brother tribal bands begin their long drift to the great summer gathering place of our people."

Expression dumbfounded, Carries-His-Lion wrenched his head sideways to glare at the wrinkled old holy man. Once again in unison, the remaining council members nodded their own heads and murmured agreement. Carries-His-Lion returned his eyes to the teepee's vent flap.

"The tribal gathering, like the summer, does not come for three moons yet. What madness is this?" Carries-His-Lion blurted out.

Ignoring the out-of-turn eruption, Pony Man spoke, his graceful storytelling tones elaborating on the two matters so far discussed by all but the outraged warrior whose conduct the council had been called for.

"Maybe the early summer speaks to us of an early winter, reminding us to prepare for our people's largest gathering which always comes before the arrival of Cold Maker's fierce storms." Pony Man's veiled eyes glanced up from the fire, briefly touching those of all but Carries-His-Lion before making their way back to the flames.

Carries-His-Lion, mouth open, stared at the old storyteller.

Why have you and this stupid old ghost man even been brought to council? Your words make only foolish noise. But mindful of his breach of council conduct moments earlier, Carries-His-Lion bit his lip and kept silent.

The circle completed, all now waited for the camp chief to begin the next round of discussion.

"Ghost Head and Pony Man speak the truth, and I thank them for their wise words. It is important to prepare for our people's great gathering. To see that all goes well for the sacred Sun Dance and the gladness of reuniting with all the others of our nation."

Carries-His-Lion looked from face to face with suspicious distrust.

"Humph!" Crow Chaser grunted, punctuating a second challenging look at his young adversary.

Lion's face turned red.

You no longer have a warrior's spirit old man. You speak words only through your ugly wife's foul mouth.

There followed another long silence.

Many Dogs shifted his injured leg, absently scratching at its knee before pulling the limb up against his chest.

"There are many temptations at the gathering, our camp police must be well prepared. They must be experienced in the many responsibilities of a tribal gathering, I think."

Lion's eyes shot to Many Dogs who was once again scratching at the knee.

Half-sized Grandmother chief!

Beaver Tail nodded, glanced sideways at Carries-His-Lion, showing a tight smile. "Yes, he said, "these things are much important."

This time Carries-His-Lion delayed, certain Beaver only feigned being done so he could interrupt him again. When the silence became uncomfortably long, he took in a breath and opened his mouth...

"How does a three-legged dog piss, anyway?" Beaver Tail wondered not quite under his breath.

Silence.

"This talk," Carries-His-Lion muttered, "it is like a stupid dog chasing its tail. It goes nowhere, it says nothing." But resolve had fled his voice.

Indirect as it was, the will of the council moved with the swelling force of a spring runoff. The aggrieved War Chief of the Lion Shadows now understood, that after this council, he and his Shadow warriors would no longer be the band's camp police.

We are to be replaced three moons early just because it is hot and these feeble-minded old men are blind to the schemes of certain women in this camp.

His head fell, chin to chest.

Ghost Head picked up a pinch of dirt from the earth beneath him and sprinkled it on the fire then spat into the flames. When the spittle quit sizzling, he spoke again.

"It is decided," the holy man declared softly. "Come, Pony Man, the council's circle must finish without the noisiness of our words." Both rose, nodding silently to the circle of seated chiefs as they left.

"Ouch," Fish's son protested as he jerked his head from beneath the teepee's skirt and scowled at Sees-The-Sky's prodding foot. He didn't have courage enough to direct that same disapproving look up at the foot's owner. She held her own glare long enough to assure all sign of his resentment had been swallowed.

"Well? What does the angry one say now?" Sees-The-Sky asked the skinny youngster.

"He pouts. A Blackfeet war party could gallop across his lip," the boy quipped.

"And the others? Speak to me, boy."

"They have agreed that Chief Beaver Tail's Yellow Wolf hunter society will be the new camp police." The young brave snickered. "The grandfathers say the Yellow Wolfs must have time to practice their camp police duties so that all might be dignified and suitable for the great tribal gathering and Sun Dance."

* * *

When Lion Hunter heard of the council decision he sat down to think about the matter. He and Kills-In-The-Dark had witnessed the camp's morning upset. He remembered now that she had quickly hurried off to call upon Ghost Head, a visit she did not allow him to accompany her on. He watched her tramp back to her own lodge afterward while the holy man hurried off among the camp's teepees on a mission of unknown importance. Lion Hunter now understood the mission. Kills-In-The-Dark had sent Ghost Head to recommend a council, one that would remove the Lion Shadows' camp policing powers and remedy the camp's problems.

He smiled to himself.

* * *

Lion Hunter had long hoped his mentor would select Wolf Ridge, the namesake of his people, as the site for his vision quest, but he had never actually journeyed to the sacred mountain that ridge was so prominently carved from. So when he found himself scaling the lushly forested slope that led to his people's most precious holy site, he was nearly overwhelmed by the profound sense of life's rightness that came over him. For the first time in memory he knew contentment, deep and mellow, and he had unshakable faith in the promise of his future.

He was breathing hard when he popped his head up over Wolf Ridge and looked around. The floor of the ledge was little more than thirty steps at its greatest depth, maybe two hundred from side to side—a large gouge out of the side of White Mountain. Lion Hunter was nearest the west end of the ledge where it narrowed to a rock-strewn path at the foot of the ledge's granite back-wall.

He pulled himself up, pivoting on his hands, then plopped his rear end down, leaving his feet dangling over the edge.

Covered in sweat, he was about to focus his full attention on the magnificence of the Great Maker's works that stretched out below when he suddenly became aware there was something in the middle of the trail not more than twenty strides from where he sat. He leapt to his feet—spinning to face whatever silent threat had come upon him and was astonished to discover two disembodied amber eyes shimmering in the air above the trail. Lion Hunter drew in a sharp breath, jerked his knife from its sheath and crouched, ready for attack.

How can there just be eyes?

As he balanced, anticipating the worst, the form of a grey-white wolf with blacked-tipped ears gradually materialized around the strange eyes, as though emerging from the speckled background of the granite wall.

The animal's deep yellow-brown eyes fixed him with unnerving intensity.

Lion Hunter assumed the animal was real, that his own eyes had played a trick upon him in their first glance. He waited, breathing once again but now in quick shallow spurts.

The wolf remained still, continuing its stare.

Are you spirit or wolf?

When the creature did not attack, the fright in Lion Hunter's taut muscles began its retreat and a jittery uneasiness overtook him—his thoughts swirled around dim images of an uncertain future.

Then, he woke up.

5

Kills-In-The-Dark walked quickly toward her teepee, her eyes scanning the surrounding paths. Except for Lion Hunter, no other villagers were within hearing—they rarely were near her lodge. She had been away from camp the entire morning, her errand a mystery to Lion Hunter.

"Hunter, come." Her whisper pressed him to follow as she hurried past his lean-to. She was already ducking through the entrance to her lodge by the time he set aside the rawhide moccasin soles he had been working on.

He didn't understand why speaking so quietly might be necessary, but he did the same, calling softly to her when he reached her teepee.

"Aunt, I have come."

"Enter. Sit," she responded, no longer whispering. "I have arranged a meeting for you with Spirit Man."

Lion Hunter looked at his mentor in shocked silence. His people had exiled the old man many years before Lion Hunter's birth. He was dead to them by custom, and his people never spoke the names of their dead. Even though Lion Hunter was sure the old man's living name had not been Spirit Man, he felt certain his mentor violated the spirit of the custom by just saying that. Speaking of him, by any name, admitted he lived.

Noting Lion Hunter's awkward silence, Kills-In-The-Dark snorted.

"Should I not speak Spirit Man's name? That is a foolish old woman's custom, not a burden I would take upon myself. Tell me, almost-warrior, if Kills-In-The-Dark speaks of the dead, do wagging tongues condemn?"

His answer was thoughtfully slow. "No," he said.

"And why is that?"

"Because you are strange and many fear there is power in that strangeness, so they do not criticize."

Kills-In-The-Dark sat quietly, a suppressed smile twitching at the good side of her mutilated mouth.

"And so?" she urged at last.

Lion Hunter paused, then decided she intended he answer her last question.

"Your power influences our people, I think."

Actually Ghost Head's words influence—but only after your tongue has given those words to his mouth.

He stuck his chin out, smugly returning her bold eye contact.

Head tilted, she studied this new boldness. After long moments, she reached up to the nearest of the five desiccated heads hanging from her lodge poll and stroked the trophy's raven-black hair with her fingertips.

"One day you will be a leader, Lion Hunter, almost-warrior—a leader who does not need to be a witch to sway others." A smile once again twitched at the corner of her mouth. "My strangeness is a thing none but Spirit Man understands. He will teach this to you because you must understand the strangeness in a person before you can understand how to guide that person."

Lion Hunter, not yet understanding the importance of her words, remained silent, instead fixing his eyes on the desiccated head whose hair she stroked, wondering again what magic these fearsome trophies made for her.

"Three days from now you will meet Spirit Man by the Grandmother Tree." She spoke louder, recapturing his wandering attention. He knew from the storyteller's tales that the Grandmother Tree was on Lodgepole Mountain, a very important mountain to his people because of the abundance of pine trees they used for their teepees. It was two days east of the Wolf Ridge village's current location.

Still uncomfortable with her indifference to tribal custom, Lion Hunter held his silence—she also withheld any facial expression.

"You will go to the Grandmother tree on Lodgepole Mountain to meet him. You will journey with him for a time," she continued, "then, when he has taught you the fox's secrets as he taught them to me, you will be ready to go on your Vision Quest and become a man."

Lion Hunter's insides exploded with excitement.

Finally, I will become a man. I will go on raids and become a famous warrior, and… but why does she say Spirit Man is the only one who understands her strangeness? Of all our people, why him?

* * *

Lion Hunter set out for the sacred mountain early the next morning, riding the black gelding that had been his father's pony but was now Kills-In-The-Dark's. He rode with bow and arrows slung across his back and lance in hand—its grip braided with white ermine skins he'd traded for his rabbit blanket. A pack containing venison jerky, spare moccasins, the sheepskin shirt his mother saved from the *Taking* for him and his fire-building needs hung over the horse's withers. Because it was so warm, he wore only his breechcloth and black-dyed deerskin leggings pulled down over calf-high moccasins. His chest, just beginning to fill out, was bare.

Sitting tall atop the gelding, he raised his chin to the wind, which brought heat up in blustery gusts from the dry lands to the south.

"We are warriors," Lion Hunter announced loudly to the gelding, but only because they were safely away from the eyes and ears of his band's camp. "I will call you Black Storm because you will carry me like thunder across the plains on great raids."

"When I am a true warrior," Lion Hunter this time shouted at the top of his lungs, "we shall count many coups together, Black Storm." The thought completed, he lapsed into silence, sitting his newly pronounced war pony with straight-backed pride.

The gravity of his journey soon found him settled into the lone plainsman's constant concern—remaining alive in the hostile world of a vast expanse of open country with little safe harbor and the constant prospect of dangerous encounters with deadly elements and enemy warriors. Lion Hunter rode the rolling landscape carefully—always remaining just below its skylines. He scanned his surroundings from the shadows of trees, gullies, or other concealed locations before moving through areas in which he might easily be discovered. He carefully avoided startling wild creatures so their frightened reactions would not alert others to his presence. These were things his father had taught him before he was ten but now, as he neared manhood, they were no longer games—they could easily be the difference between life and death and he realized that.

The first day was blustery. Tumbling gusts of wind pummeled his back so often he had to tie back his long hair to keep it from lashing around into his face and eyes. Dust clouds blew up frequently, causing Black Storm to shy sideways twice. He was nearly unseated both times.

He ate while riding, not wanting to stop early in the day. It was late afternoon when he finally dropped down into an eroded channel to set up camp near a stunted bramble of serviceberry shrubs with a seep-water pool and suitable graze for his pony, nearby.

He hobbled the pony then, searched the surrounding brush until he found a good throwing stick for rabbit hunting and set out to make a kill. Dusk approached, and while the meatier jackrabbits would be coming out to graze on the plain he saw several cottontails already out and nibbling on grass in the gully. He wanted to please Spirit Man tomorrow by arriving with fresh meat.

I think maybe grandfather's teeth are not strong enough for jerky.

Lion Hunter killed two cottontails, stunning them with accurate tosses before snatching them up to snap their necks. Prior to cleaning them he ceremonially laid their limp bodies out on the grass and thanked them for giving up their lives so that he and Spirit Man might nourish their spirits while visiting the Grandmother Tree.

Early the next morning, Lion Hunter carefully scattered sign of his presence. He mounted the gelding and urged it up out of the runoff. From above, he turned and carefully inspected the campsite. Satisfied with his effort, he continued on.

By the next morning, the wind had died to little more than a breeze. He now traveled through a range of undisturbed, gently rippling grass for as far as he could see and his concern for being discovered became constant.

No buffalo or elk have come this way to churn up the earth. Here, I will leave a straight trail to where ever I make my camp.

He began riding at the base of ridges where rock debris gathered after falling from farther upslope. The rubble inhibited grass growth and made his passage less evident. Elk and other oft-used game trails, when he came across them, became more important in the thick grass, not only to ease passage but also to obscure his passage. He turned

Black Storm to them even when they took him far out of his way.

Lion Hunter decided he wouldn't stop until after dark. Only then would he carefully sneak back, paralleling his trail, to camp within hearing of where he had passed.

He rode easier after that but remained alert to the behavior of soaring birds and carefully watched for distant dust clouds and smoke, both signs other humans may be nearby.

Shortly after nightfall, beneath pre-moon starlight, he spotted the gray shadow of Lodgepole Mountain and decided to make camp. Kills-In-The-Dark had given him good directions.

Lion Hunter turned his pony off trail, dropped down into a small streambed and dismounted, leaving the black shadow of the channel wall between his intended campsite and Lodgepole Mountain's broad apron.

"Black Storm," he said scratching the pony's rump as it muzzled into the streambed's shallow water, "you must be content without wandering tonight. I need you close by so you can tell me if others approach."

When Black Storm was done, Lion Hunter led it downstream paralleling his back trail. It worried him that the pony's splashing-rock-clacking steps in the streambed seemed to echo into the next night.

Lion Hunter stopped when he found a spot where they were sure to hear any riders who might pass during the night.

"We will set our camp in this dry place," Lion Hunter told Black Storm as he dropped his pack and weapons and removed the gelding's halter. He stood by proudly, watching as his pony shook, first head, then body, before sucking in a great draft of air and letting it pour back out with a long sigh. Black Storm looked back at Lion Hunter for a moment, let out a soft nicker, then snatched up a tuft of grass and began chomping contentedly.

Shuffling through the surrounding grass, Lion Hunter searched for river stones by feeling with his feet. Those he found he tossed out into the stream, continuing until the tiny glade was clear of all but a few last stones. Those remaining he piled next to his pack, to be used later for a small fire ring.

"The sound of your hooves clacking on rock travels far in darkness," he explained to the pony as he hobbled its legs together to keep it from wandering.

Satisfied his camp was concealed well enough, Lion Hunter climbed the channel's bank and settled into the shadow of a cottonwood overhang—darker than the surrounding night. He made sure he could see the pony, a deep black shadow below him, before shifting his gaze to the pale rise of Lodgepole Mountain's gray apron to his right. He looked for the Grandmother Tree's black silhouette but could not distinguish it from the others that populated the mountain's thickly forested slopes.

The night breeze was pleasant, and it felt good to lean back against the tree's trunk and let his eyes close.

"Hey, ya, young Lion Hunter, you are well?"

Lion Hunter sprang to his feet, heart pounding. Down in the gully, Spirit Man's thin shadow stood next to that of Black Storm—his grey hair ghostly white in the moonlight. The pony had its muzzle in the old man's outstretched hand, and the sounds of its contented chomping suddenly burst into Lion Hunter's consciousness. He should have already alerted to that sound.

Old man, you annoy me. I do not wish you to feed my pony oats so you can sneak up on me.

When the horse finished the last of its treat, Spirit Man patted its neck affectionately and tilted his head up to Lion Hunter.

"Ponies live always in my heart," he whispered loudly, "but they make much noise. It is a sad thing that a dead man's journeys must always be silent, so he does not become more dead. Anyway, I walk," Spirit Man lamented, scratching the pony's outstretched nose.

Still unsettled by the old man's startling appearance, Lion Hunter made no reply.

"We cannot journey with a pony," Spirit Man continued. "They step too noisily and make loud whinnies to others of their kind."

Lion Hunter rallied his pride, slid down the bank, and walked up to the exile.

"I have come from Kills-In-The-Dark's lodge, Grandfather."

Lion Hunter briefly lowered his eyes in respect, and then looked the old man up and down. He was surprised to discover he had grown taller than Spirit Man. He last saw Spirit Man two years before, when he was fourteen—the year he killed the cut-nosed lioness and took the name, Lion Hunter. Spirit Man himself had suggested the name after startling him with a sudden appearance, just like tonight. That happened shortly after the kill. Lion Hunter examined the old man as well as darkness allowed.

Who makes such fine clothing for you if you are dead to our people? And why do you creep up to surprise me when you have come to meet me anyway?

After an uncomfortable pause, Lion Hunter asked politely, "Am I to make a journey with you, Grandfather?"

"You have been sent to make two journeys with me. The first is to learn the early living times of Kills-In-The-Dark and how she came to have such a name. The second is to learn the secrets of the fox and other wild creatures. Kills-In-The-Dark asked me to teach you these things so you can become an important warrior to your people."

With that, the old man lapsed into silence, absently reaching into his pocket and pulling out another handful of oats. While Black Storm, muzzle in hand, munched the grain, the old man gently leaned his forehead against its nose. Lion Hunter watched, seeing Spirit Man's nostrils flare as he drew in the horse's powerful scent, a joy long ago ripped from him by his exile. Lion Hunter could not imagine a life without ponies.

Several times in the past, Lion Hunter had been similarly startled by the old man's sudden appearances, each while he was alone and away from his village. The first time, Lion Hunter had stood frozen like a rabbit upon discovering the old man sitting cross legged no more than a few steps from him.

On that occasion, Spirit Man helped him track and find a wounded deer. The animal bolted just as Lion Hunter loosed his arrow. Gut-shot, the panicked creature fled into the thick brambles of a north-facing slope, leaving so little blood and disturbance that Lion Hunter was unable to find where it laid up. Filled with shame, he dreaded admitting his failure to his father. It was not just that his shot missed its mark. His shame was for the wounded animal's suffering, for the waste of its meat, and most of all because he was unable to thank the creature for the gift of its life. It was from the gloom of this shame that Lion Hunter looked up those years ago, to discover Spirit Man sitting nearby, quietly watching him.

"I smell rabbit," Spirit Man said abruptly.

Lion Hunter jolted back to the present.

"Yes, Grandfather, I have brought fresh roasted rabbit. I thought you might have hunger."

"You make a good gift to this old, dead man. I think I shall find gladness in our journey together."

Lion Hunter smiled. Annoyed or not, the old man's praise felt good.

While the two ate, Spirit Man told Lion Hunter his plans.

"We first go to Grandmother," he announced. "Do you see her?" he pointed. "She is there on that ridge. Near that first saddle—the tallest."

With Spirit Man's help, Lion Hunter found the grand old pine's dark shadow quickly. The tree was not just taller but broader than all the shadows surrounding it.

"Her roots are said to reach to the center of Earth-Mother," Spirit Man continued. "They were used as guides by the first people who climbed out into this real world."

"Young Pigeon," Spirit Man continued, "was taken slave by the Blackfeet beneath Grandmother's sacred limbs." He paused, eyeing Lion Hunter, who looked confused.

"Aha," Spirit Man teased, "so you thought your mentor, Kills-In-The-Dark, did not have a child name like the rest of our people. Well, she did. She was a pretty child so your true grandfather, Lion Hunter, my best friend, honored her with a pretty name—Pigeon."

Lion Hunter looked away, embarrassed at having been read so easily. Spirit Man reached out and gently laid his gnarled hand on Lion Hunter's shoulder before continuing.

"After I have told you the story of her new name, we will return your pony to the village herd so our journey can be quiet like a shadow. We cannot sneak up and lie with the sleeping deer if we journey with a pony stepping on the ground like thunder." He smiled, dark eyes lost amid deep shadowed wrinkles.

* * *

Midmorning the next day, Lion Hunter, leading his pony, climbed the stream bank to where Spirit Man stood looking at the towering mountain. He stopped next to the old man, gazing in the same direction trying to locate in daylight the tree that was today's destination. Out of respect he held back many questions about being sent to the wilderness.

Spirit Man abruptly cocked his head to one side, swiveling his eyes upward to watch the growing form of an approaching raven. It soared into view from the east while venting a series of excited caws. In moments, a second raven appeared from the same direction, flapping its wings hard, trying to catch up to the first. This one gave a single call to its mate, which had begun circling toward Lodgepole Mountain. The soft compression sounds of the mate's wing beats could be heard even from this distance over the morning hush of the plains.

"Come, Lion Hunter. Something strange happens. A hunting, I think."

Spirit Man scrambled farther up the rise, reaching its highest point before returning his attention to the ravens—both were now soaring in a circle overhead. Lion Hunter heard his pony making nervous movements and, out of habit, hesitated to look back and gauge its behavior. Head held high, the animal was snorting and scenting the air. Lion Hunter's own senses ignited.

Something is about to happen or… is happening.

Quickly climbing to the high spot, he joined Spirit Man in squinting against the growing breeze, watching the ravens as they began circling, now over a stream at the base of the big mountain's skirt.

Four more ravens appeared, these coming from the west. The two groups converged over the gradually rising mountain skirt—a parched area of barren scrub sage below the mountain's dark forest line farther up the mountain.

At first he and Spirit Man saw nothing more, then three large animals appeared below them, loping up out of one of the constant depressions on this part of the plain.

They were grizzlies, a sow and twin yearlings crossing between the two Indians and the stream. They were moving toward the mountain's skirt. The mother had been frequently looking over her shoulder but suddenly stopped, whirled and reared up on her hind legs, nose lifted to the wind. She appeared anxious. The yearlings, looking uncertain, stopped and turned back toward their mother. Lion Hunter could feel the fear in them.

They were last year's cubs, each easily twice Lion Hunter's size. Together the three would make a terrifying force against any enemy. Their alarm made little sense to Lion Hunter. Apprehension swept over him.

"Why are these bears so afraid, Grandfather?" he whispered to Spirit Man. "Does a big male bear chase them?"

"Something worse, I think. Look, the ravens circle over them now."

The sow dropped back to all fours, spun back around and hurried past her two cubs. They raced to catch up, then tucked themselves into the safety of their mother's flanks and resumed nervous lopes. All three now repeatedly glanced over their shoulders.

"She knows what enemy chases her family but not because she scents them. The wind is in her face. Her young smell the fear in their mother, so they, too, are afraid," the old man explained.

The three fleeing grizzlies crossed below Lion Hunter and Spirit Man, splashed through the stream, and began climbing the mountain's apron. The mountain's tree line and the safety of its forest loomed in the distance.

Three smaller figures, long and sleek, bounded up out of the depression fresh on the bears' track—wolves, moving faster than the bears, but not yet in full pursuit. A large black wolf led with two grays trailing at its flanks. The ravens chattered, their excitement growing as the bears suddenly began sprinting.

Moments later, more wolves silently loped up out of the depression—then more and still others, nineteen in all. The remainder of the pack began true pursuit, spreading out as they skirted the stream bank. Rapt, Lion Hunter stood watching the shrinking space behind the retreating bears and their pursuers. For the first time he feared for the bears' lives.

"Grandfather, this is strange. Why does the wolf family chase this bear mother and her young?"

"I know these wolves. The black is their leader and this is his hunting, I think." He shook his head slowly.

The lead wolves put on a burst of speed, now stretched out in full pursuit. The three bears, instantly panicked, racing at breakneck speed toward the distant tree line, but they were rapidly overtaken. Lion Hunter knew they would be caught—the safety of the mountain's forest was too far away.

The remaining ravens arrived overhead, and the excitement of the group's calls flooded the surrounding plain while the deadly scene being played out below them continued in ominous silence. The hair on Lion Hunter's neck stood up.

The smaller of the two yearlings, gawking back over its shoulder at the fast approaching wolves, bumped into its mother's shoulder and pitched into a tumbling ball of sprawling legs and uprooted brush.

The panicked creature came up, limbs still scrambling, running even faster as it bawled at the retreating backsides of its mother and larger sibling.

The mother bear, reacting to her yearling's cry, skidded to a stop and scrabbled around with an outraged bellow to confront the oncoming threat to her family. The three leading wolves slowed, grays ranging out to either side of the desperate sow while the big black began a stiff-legged walk toward her, mane bristling, head low and threatening—no trace of fear in its approach.

The rest of the pack split, sprinting past the first three wolves and bristling mother grizzly, launching their own attacks on the two inexperienced yearlings.

For just a moment the sow's head tensely jerked back and forth between the three wolves that menaced her and those now attacking her young. She dropped her forelegs back to the earth and, abandoning her confrontation with the black, spun and raced off to defend her offspring. All three wolves responded by lunging at her rear legs, slashing and darting away as she alternately spun to knock them away then resume her desperate attempt to reach her young.

Though twice the size of any one of their attackers, each yearling was engulfed by its own mass of relentlessly attacking wolves whose vicious ripping assaults came simultaneously from many directions. Fangs cut into sinew and flesh as powerful jaws time and again clamped down, violently tearing great bloody wounds into the flanks and legs of the bawling pair of yearlings.

The enraged mother bear stormed into the writhing cluster of wolves that were attacking the smaller of the two cubs. Powerful blows from her massive paws sent three wolves yelping as they hurtled through the air. One, body broken, crashed to the earth and did not rise—the other two were up immediately rushing back into the fray. The rest, having momentarily darted out of reach, renewed their furious onslaught.

Gnashing her powerful jaws, she repeatedly lunged at them from a protective stance over the cub. Her attempts found only air as the wolves scurried ceaselessly about her. They feigned attack each time she faced them, sunk fangs into her flesh or that of the cub's when she did not, their blood-spattered muzzles almost smiling one moment, twisted into savage snarls the next.

The sow grizzly's repeated attempts to protect its gravely injured yearling were failing. In a last effort, the terrified cub lurched to its feet and, with a wolf still clinging to its flesh, abandoned its mother and began a desperate dash for the safety of the tree line. The ravaged creature was quickly overtaken and hauled back to the earth, bawling piteously as the last of its courage wilted. Unable to rise, the dying cub was again engulfed by attackers, its flesh shredded by bloody fangs from every direction. Inexperienced and used to its mother's protection, the cub gave up all resistance, shrieking out in fear as the wolves shouldered in to finish it off.

The sow, reacting to her smallest's death cries, smashed aside the wolf nearest her, knocking the attacker through the air whimpering with pain. She raced to the yearling, ignoring the wolves slashing at her haunches. Eight wolves, their muzzles red with gore, scattered as she approached but returned immediately, only to renew their attack, now on her, and from all directions. The mortally wounded cub was reduced to whimpering, but the mother, standing over its mangled body, could only defend herself. She had no time to render motherly care to her offspring.

The sow's larger yearling still brawled ferociously against the onslaught of the rest of the pack. It fought silently, unrelenting in its own savagery against the endless tide of its attackers. When the overwhelming weight of them bore it to the ground also, several wolves that had been attacking the mother rushed to join in its slaughter.

The beleaguered sow tried to respond to the killing of her larger yearling but was forced to turn back to the smaller when the remaining wolves renewed their butchery of its limp form. Hopelessly, she returned to straddle the smaller cub's body, her sides heaving, shielding at least this one against further attack.

She looked on helpless, swinging her huge head back and forth between the wolves surrounding her and the deadly brawl engulfing her larger yearling. All lost, she stretched her neck out and bawled mournfully, a lingering cry full of a mother's despair.

Her awful cry tolled the end of the massacre.

The wolves, panting heavily, withdrew from the carnage, gathering around three of their own fallen members, nosing their limp bodies and whimpering. Eventually, those still living moved to secure distances from the gore-strewn battleground and the three grizzlies. They assumed placid positions—some lying, others sitting, most licked wounds while the rest remained idle licking gore from their coats. All faced the grizzly sow, gazing at her impassively.

Bear and wolf alike understood the hunt had come to its end. The pack, even with its superior numbers, could not absorb the huge loss an attempt to slay the sow would cause.

For a moment all remained in utter silence, then something unexpected happened.

The larger yearling, which had lain without moving, abruptly stirred. Struggling desperately, the cub gained its feet and stood wobbling as the wolves watched renewed curiosity burning in their eyes. Sunlight glinted from the yearling's blood-sopped coat, its face was destroyed, and its belly was ripped open so widely guts trailed down between its legs. The pathetic creature, trembling with weakness, lifted its nose to the wind and upon finding its mother's scent turned its sightless head in her direction. The ruined animal completed a single step toward her then collapsed back to the earth and ceased all movement.

A raven brazenly swooped to the ground and began investigating the cub's carcass—burying its head in the gapping belly wound. Two others landed nearby, hopping about warily while the rest watched from farther away.

The black wolf rose, looking intently at the fallen yearling. When no further movement occurred, it turned its gaze to the sow which, head drooping, returned a listless stare. The black walked to the cub's carcass, bent and sniffed at it before lifting his head again and looking back at the distraught sow. The wolf paused briefly to glance at the raven, which quickly skipped away, then deliberately fitted its mouth to the dead yearling's throat and shook it savagely.

Its need satisfied, the big alpha turned and trotted off in the direction from which all had come. The remaining wolves rose and, after briefly sniffing at their dead, mutely trotted off behind the black, three of them limping.

The raven, waiting until the wolves were a safe distance away, cocked its head, momentarily appraising the bear, then hopped back to the carcass, and returned to its gory feast. The remaining ravens quickly swooped down and joined it. Looking on dully, the sow allowed her massive body to sink to the ground. There, she licked briefly at her smallest yearling's wounds before lowering her chin to the backs of her paws to stare up at the distant tree line.

"Grandfather, what has happened?"

"This we can discover when we walk in the wolf family's tracks," the old man responded over his shoulder. He was already walking toward the site of the killing.

6

While the old man walked toward the kill site, Lion Hunter stood gazing at his back in dismay.

Why do you not wait for me to get my pony, Grandfather? Your ways are strange.

But it was the thoughts of the bear killings that flooded his mind as he hurried back to where he had left the horse and his other belongings.

The wolves had not attacked the bears for food. Lion Hunter understood it the moment they withdrew from the slaughter. This seemed odd to Lion Hunter, who did not understand why a wolf family would hunt down and kill a large predator and then leave without eating. And the wolves had lost three of their number during the attack, a terrible loss to their family.

These things did not fit the ways of wolves, at least as Lion Hunter knew them. His people revered wolves for their intelligence and strong family loyalties. All wolves, even those forced by the pack to eat and lay apart from the rest, lived under the close protection of the family. Packs of wolves often skirmished with more powerful predators at kill sites, but the family's safety always came first. Lion Hunter had heard many stories of packs giving up kills to aggressive grizzlies and even once to a wolverine not so large as the smallest female wolf.

Lion Hunter continued mulling over the puzzling attack as he gathered his weapons and pack, untied the horsehair hobble from Black Storm's legs, and set out to catch up to his mentor.

"You can ride on Black Storm and I will walk, Grandfather." Lion Hunter threw his leg over the pony's neck and slid his bottom down over its shoulder landing sure-footed next to the old man. He preferred dismounting that way because it made him feel like a real warrior. His father had taught him to do this as the horse still moved—

the way warriors did during the fast moving confusion of battle.

Spirit Man waved off the offer without comment. Shrugging, Lion Hunter fell into step beside the old man, leaving the pony to trail behind on its own. They dropped into the depression and began walking toward the kill site. Near the stream they found damp earth and sweet-grass tufts. Lion Hunter's pony was again becoming edgy, so Spirit Man told Lion Hunter to leave it behind.

Tightness grew in Lion Hunter's stomach as the two crossed the stream and moved up the apron, toward the grieving mother bear.

The old man spoke softly.

"When we are close enough to make her nervous she will look in other directions to see what other danger is near. We will stop then, and sit. Do not look directly into her eyes. She knows we come but does not know why. She will watch and if we do not further threaten, her concern will cool."

"Yes, Grandfather." Lion Hunter noted a soft breeze scuttling over the raised hair on his neck.

"We will sit and watch from the corners of our eyes while I speak to you of some things."

"Yes, Grandfather."

The mother bear was still lying over the remains of her smallest cub. Lion Hunter and Spirit Man were close enough to see her nostrils flaring when she lifted her huge head and began glancing about in other directions.

With casualness he did not feel, Lion Hunter lowered himself to the grass facing Spirit Man who, after lowering himself, sat quietly gazing off along the wolves' back trail.

A few steps away from the huge sow and her smallest, the ravens squabbled amongst themselves contesting feasting rights at the larger yearling's carcass.

Lion Hunter, who could feel the sow's small black eyes boring into him, battled the onset of fear. He knew she, like all scent hunters, could smell fear—it was part of the hunter's heart.

I must be brave.

He began thinking of his father, seeing the proud warrior sitting upon his favorite war pony, looking down over the Wolf Ridge people's camp. Lion Hunter imagined himself mounted on Black Storm while sitting at his father's side, and that both were fierce protectors of their people.

"Hunter," the old man said, his words soft and relaxed, "during the wolves' attack she feared only for her young. She fought them without fear for herself. It is the same with us. She has no fear of us, just caution. She does not see us as food for her belly. She watches us only to understand our meaning. After a short time, she will decide she does not understand why we are here and that will make her nervous to leave. She knows that her young cannot be harmed anymore. If she did not, she would chase the ravens away."

"I understand, Grandfather." Being dragged away from his brave-fantasy troubled him. He did not yet feel brave.

"The she-bear again makes quick looks in other directions, but we do not threaten. Soon, her spirit will tell her it is unwise to stay longer because she does not understand our meaning. She is deciding what direction is best for her. When she stands, we will stand also but we must wait until she has turned her head again. We must both rise at the same time and look directly into her eyes.

"Do you understand?"

"Yes." Lion Hunter gripped his hands together to keep Spirit Man from seeing them shake.

"If we move toward her before she turns away, or if we crouch or hunch forward like another predator, she will see a threat in our actions. These are always the positions of creatures who are hungry and of those who hunt others. Do you understand what I have said?"

"Yes, Grandfather. But if we stand and look at her, will she not see a threat then?"

"No. She will see only our interest, and that will make her nervous because she does not understand that interest. She will be anxious to leave. She prepares to rise, are you ready?"

Lion Hunter nodded, straining his eyes at their periphery. The she-bear held both of them steadily in her gaze, her breathing so heavy Lion Hunter imagined he could feel the heat of it.

"We stand now."

Both slowly stood, the sow mirroring their movements by lifting her own massive form up to a threatening crouch.

Lion Hunter locked his knees in place to prevent them from shaking. Oddly, Lion Hunter noticed a blade of buffalograss, drool-stuck to her wet nose.

"Look directly into her eyes, Lion Hunter. Stand straight and do not move."

Holding his breath, Lion Hunter chomped down on his lip. He still could not look into her eyes.

"Almost warrior, it is time to be a man now. I am afraid also, but she is looking for a reason to leave—to move away from what she does not understand, and we must give her that reason now. She understands when others fear her—her totem is more powerful than all others in the real world. But she does not understand when others are not frightened. Look now."

Shamed by Spirit Man's reminder, Lion Hunter slid his eyes sideways, resolutely staring into the enormous creature's unblinking black eyes.

All three stood silently, staring for several moments before Lion Hunter realized she had begun to slowly lift her bulk into a full standing position.

"She stands up tall now," Spirit Man said out loud. "She is still nervous but does not feel threatened. Watch her head and eyes. They will tell us when to move."

She broke off her stare long enough to swivel her head, glancing to the side and rear before once again fixing her full attention on them. One of the feasting ravens suddenly lifted into flight, bright sunlight glinting from its black feathers. The she-bear jerked her massive head in its direction and most of the rest scattered. Those that did not hopped quickly away from the carcass, nervously watching the bear.

"She checks for a safe way to leave. Do not move or look away yet."

The bear made several nervous body movements as though beginning to turn away, but each time she changed her mind and returned her tense attention to the two men standing before her. She flexed her jaw sideways. Long strings of slobber dripped from her sagging lips as she stood measuring them.

A long pause, then, head still warily facing the two, she turned her shoulders and began sidestepping away. Spirit

Man let her take several more of these guarded steps before he took a stride in the direction of the yearling she just abandoned.

Startled, the sow broke into a stumbling run, suddenly lurching sideways when the remaining ravens burst into the air at her shoulder. Twenty steps away she came to a hesitant stop and turned around, anxiously shifting her attention between the two humans and the flustered birds.

Upon reaching the smaller yearling's carcass, the old man lowered himself to the ground and, eyes still alertly engaging those of the mother bear, bent his head down as though beginning to feed.

"She sees that I am claiming the carcass of her dead cub," Spirit Man said to Lion Hunter. "The she-bear has no interest in eating her young, and she does not see me as food so I am fooling her into making a food-decision instead of a defending-herself decision or a defending-her-young decision. She will leave now, I think. But we will not stay long. Her bear totem is mighty, and she will return soon when her spirit reminds her that she is a mother—a grizzly mother."

The reek of bear was overwhelming.

Is her scent so strong because I have fear or because she is so near?

"Memorize this grizzly stink, Hunter," Spirit Man cautioned. "They are shrewd and dangerous. Remembering could save your life one day."

The mother bear reluctantly began moving away again as Lion Hunter watched, but was still in sight when she stopped and once again turned back to stare steadily in their direction.

"It is time to leave now, I think. Her mother spirit is beginning to call to her again."

The two climbed back to their feet, the old man pausing to study the distant animal's posture while Lion Hunter, shifting from foot to foot, darted nervous looks between his strange new mentor and the ominous she-bear. Any delay was too long for him.

"Grandfather, should we go?"

Spirit Man turned to Lion Hunter, his grey, almost white, hair ringing an ancient face alive with excitement.

Why do you do this crazy thing, old man? I do not understand you.

"Yes, we go now." Spirit Man responded, and the two set off walking back toward the swale where they had left Black Storm. As they neared the stream, Lion Hunter was relieved to find his pony standing calm, ears forward, looking up at them from the meadow.

Lion Hunter resisted the gripping urge to turn back one last time to see what the bear was doing. He moved quickly, passing Spirit Man, whose movement was deliberate. Lion Hunter was already mounted when the old man caught up to him.

Maybe he does not fear dying because he is already dead.

They walked in silence following the wolves' back trail. It was a long while before they neared the top of the next rise. For Lion Hunter, it was a fearsome time. He felt certain the sow was behind them every step of the way, and he was desperate to look back, if only so he could know to run before the enraged beast caught up to them. He imagined he heard her labored breathing and the lumbering sounds of her charge. He even thought he could smell her foul breath but still the old man walked, unhurried, saying nothing.

Finally, Spirit Man paused to turn back to see what the mother grizzly was doing. Lion Hunter's chest muscles were still so tight he hushed his breathing so that the old man would not know the depth of his fear. He was glad he could now turn and assure himself of their safety.

The mother bear had returned to the kill site. They watched as she wearily moved to the carcass of her largest yearling, head drooping down to nudge its carcass. She scattered the feasting ravens with a listless swipe, sniffed at what remained of her dead yearling, then stood silently staring back at the mountain's distant tree line.

* * *

"I do not understand. Why did we chase the she-bear away and pretend to eat her young, Grandfather?"

"It was a learning time for an almost-warrior. A warrior must know the thinkings of the animal people before he can understand them and teach others to respect them. It is something a warrior and leader must know. It helps you to understand people, their fears, and their other concerns."

With that the old man lapsed back into silence, examining the ground before him as he walked.

A memory flash came to Lion Hunter—his mentor suddenly standing up before Carries-His-Lion during the *shaming* the confrontation.

Three lumbering bears and many wolves had traveled this same trail, so it was easy to follow. Spirit Man found blood regularly along the way and once found a spot where several of the pack had gathered around an injured companion. The hurt animal had been galloping on three legs since leaving the kill site, trying to keep up with the pack.

"The she-wolf loses much blood," Spirit Man said. "Her pack gathers to tell her goodbye. We will find her before we find the mystery of the wolf hunt, I think."

"How do you know it is a she-wolf, Grandfather?"

"Her paws are not so big as a male's, and she leaves tracks not so deep."

A short while later, they found her. She was a beautiful grey-white creature, but her left hind leg was ruined. Flesh bulged from its gaping wound, and the jagged end of a shattered bone protruded through the meat. She panted shallowly. She had collapsed on her side in the cool shade of a cottonwood. Not yet dead but too weak even to lift her head, the poor animal rolled her yellow eyes sideways, mutely watching their approach.

"The others have left her alone to die. I do not know why. Something makes them hurry on, maybe." He assessed the dying animal's reaction to the two of them for long moments before saying, "She will die with us. We will be her family, and then, when her spirit has made its journey to the Great Maker, we will go to discover the mystery of this hunt. Before the morning is done, I think."

* * *

Lion Hunter, responding to Black Storm's sudden halt and fidgety behavior, opened his senses, reaching out for any unusual change of the normal patterns of plains life while immediately looking in the direction the pony's eyes and ears had fixed upon.

"Lion Hunter, do you hear? The meadowlark makes no song here. See the large dark spots in the pine branches at the forest edge? They are too far away for my old eyes, tell me what you see."

"They are vultures, Grandfather. But Storm senses something closer."

"Yes, and there is a too-big shadow next to that boulder at the ravine wall. What do you see there?"

"It is the entrance to a den, Grandfather," Lion Hunter responded, scanning the surrounding area for wolves. He found none.

"Yes. The wolf family has been watching us. We have found the place of the hunt's beginning."

The midday sun broiled down out of the cloudless sky. The surrounding insects, already adapted to their presence, renewed their buzzing, but still no bird sang or moved.

"The family will not be ready to hunt now, but it is better that Black Storm comes with us."

"Grandfather, how do you know this is the place?"

"The wolf family is here. It is better if you ride. They have seen many of our kind riding and will see a man-pony, not just a pony and not just two men. It is safer."

"But those who attack grizzlies will not fear one man-pony and a walking grandfather, will they?"

"The wolf family fears no one, Lion Hunter. Like the grizzly they flee what they do not understand. Now, let us go and see what has caused this killing."

They approached the den's shadowed entrance and several members of the pack became visible, climbing to their feet from various shaded spots among the surrounding trees. Most moved away nervously, glancing back over their shoulders.

The huge black, lying nearest to the den entrance, looked uneasy but seemed not yet willing to move. The scene around him was as tragic as the earlier killing had been.

Bloody clumps of fur were scattered as far away as twenty strides from the den, most still attached to tangled shreds of flesh, no one piece identifiable as a whole creature. Clouds of insects attacked each in noisy celebration of their gruesome banquet. Mounds of dirt lay outside the destroyed den's entrance, and huge raking claw marks in the earth clearly identified the bears as those responsible for pillaging its precious contents.

"The Black One stays next to all that is left of his mate," Spirit Man whispered. "Just as the she-bear stays next to her dead cubs."

The black wolf rose as they made their approach. The animal moved a short distance away, then stopped, its body still facing away while it looked back over its shoulder at the two of them. Spirit Man inspected the area near the den and returned to Lion Hunter, who had remained mounted and at a distance. Black Storm, ears forward, turned his head sideways, watching the black.

"The wolf family was away when the bears found this den. The brave she-wolf fought with the large yearling, a male, I think. He came too close to her den, and she attacked him to save her young but the she-bear came quick and killed her. She, too, protected her young." Spirit Man shook his head, his face sad. "Both cubs play-killed this brave she-wolf when the mother finished shaking her." Spirit Man gazed up at Lion Hunter, his mouth tight set.

"But the male yearling smelled the den and dug out the pups. Both cubs play-killed some more with the little ones," he continued.

"The bears were gone when the rest of the wolf family came back—wolf tracks are on top, bear tracks underneath." Spirit Man jutted his chin out, indicating a confusion of prints in the dirt surrounding the den.

"The black left soon with two others. See his big prints and two others there?" Again he pointed with his chin. "But the three came back when no others followed. The others were not anxious to join this unhappy hunt. But he is the warrior of their family and he went to have his face licked by many to remind them he was their leader, and they all went with him."

Lion Hunter swiveled his eyes, finding the big male, still standing, pink tongue lolling as he panted in the midday sun. Fleeting movements among the surrounding bushes also caught his eyes, as others of the family moved about, made nervous by his and Spirit Man's continued presence.

"These things that have been done today are sad things, Lion Hunter. But they have been done, so all who survive them must now live with what is left behind. I, in my before time, when I was alive, did something that made others live with what I left behind. It is a long sadness to my life that this is so. Now, both the she-grizzly and the black warrior-wolf will find this same sadness in their lives, I think."

With that, the old man turned back toward Lodgepole Mountain, and, resuming the silence that was his habit to travel in, he set off at a brisk pace.

As they moved away, Lion Hunter turned back and watched the surrounding brush come alive with wolves rushing to the den site to sniff at each place the old walking-man and man-pony had visited.

On their journey to the Grandmother tree, Lion Hunter silently wondered what larger understanding Kills-In-The-Dark's *think-habit* could make out of the strange happenings of this day. Before, he thought he understood both creatures, but now he was sure there was much more he did not know. He remembered that Spirit Man told him he would be taught the secrets of the fox. He no longer doubted there were still many secrets to learn—many things his father did not have time to teach him before he was murdered. For now, questions whirled in his head like a devil wind.

To stop the whirling, he forced himself to think about something else. That something else was Willow, the gentle young girl who had caught his eye as he walked about the Wolf Ridge village on his mentor's errands. Her father was lamed in a hunting accident, and her family now humbled by the warrior's inability to provide for them. Camp Chief Weasel Bear, Lion Hunter's father, and others often took handouts to her family after successful hunts. Few mothers would want their son to take so poor a young woman as wife.

I am poor also. Is this why you smile at me, Willow? Because we are the same?

He shook away the discomfort of that thought, shifting instead to the last time he saw her. Her hair was neatly braided, hanging down over square shoulders, and when the two of them exchanged brief looks she wore a smile as big and perfect as all happiness. Lion Hunter's heart leaped.

Unwittingly he sat straighter on Black Storm, smiling broadly.

I will return to our village a man and take you as my wife.

He imagined himself presenting her with enough buffalo hides to make a fine teepee, holding her close in his arms.

7

Hunter and Spirit Man walked the rest of the day, arriving at the Grandmother tree before sunset.

Placing his hand on the weathered bark and staring up into the tree's canopy, Lion Hunter asked, "How old is this tree, Grandfather?"

"I do not know. It was here before our people made their journey to the real world. You know the story, yes?"

"I have heard Pony Man tell it many times."

"Take care of your pony, then I will tell you Kills-In-The-Dark's naming story."

Lion Hunter unloaded his personal items from Black Sky, led the pony to some graze, and strapped its legs with a hobble to keep it from wandering. Back beneath the big tree he sat down cross-legged facing Spirit Man.

Before the old man could begin telling his story, Lion Hunter ventured a second question.

"Grandfather, can I ask something about the wolves?"

"You have thought long about what happened." The old man smiled, nodding.

"Yes, but I do not understand the black wolf's meaning in hunting the grizzlies. Did he want revenge for the killing of his mate and pups?"

Spirit Man pondered the question for some moments before responding.

"His meaning was not so simple."

Spirit Man thought a while longer, smoothing the wrinkles out of the front of his soft leather shirt and setting aside the small shoulder bag he always carried. Lion Hunter waited. Again, he noticed the excellent workmanship of the old man's fringed shirt and wondered about it. The moccasins too were fine, but cut differently than his people customarily cut theirs.

They are Crow moccasins, maybe.

Finally, the old man cleared his throat.

"The sign around the wolf den told me the she-wolf left her pups to lure the bears away. The big bear cub was proud of his size and challenged the wolf mother. The she-wolf scrapped with him, but the mother grizzly quickly came to help her cub and the two grizzlies killed the mother wolf. Afterward, the two grizzly cubs found the den and the mother bear let them kill the wolf pups.

"This mother grizzly and the wolves will live in this same country for the many years of their lives. If she returns and allows her cubs to destroy the wolf family's pups every two or three years, there soon will be no wolf family. The mother bear will not allow her cubs to kill wolf pups again, I think. Maybe the big black understood this in his heart and fought for all the wolf families that would come in future times. Or maybe he had no understanding in his heart at all, just fierceness."

Lion Hunter sat quietly, staring absently at the last of the day's sun—thinking. When he asked nothing more on the subject, Spirit Man began the story of Kills-In-The-Dark.

"Many years ago before the summer gathering of all the bands of our tribe, young Pigeon and her family left the Wolf Ridge village to go and visit the Red Earth band. Pigeon was fourteen winters, and they wished to find a husband for her.

"But a Blackfeet war party found them camped here at Grandmother. After the Blackfeet warriors killed the rest of her family, they took Pigeon as a slave. Days later, from far away, I saw the war party with a captive riding north but I did not know then that they attacked our people or that their captive was Pigeon. I tracked the Blackfeet back-trail and found her family dead and left for the ravens.

"For the next moon I tracked the war party. I traveled far to the north until I discovered the empty site where this war party's village had been. When I returned to our land, I told your father what happened.

"In the following years, your father and his Badger warriors raided into Blackfeet country this time and that, but never found that band of Blackfeet or Pigeon. All of her family, except one, was dead so she was soon forgotten.

"For the next three winters, when our people gathered at the summer tribal meets and I could not be near them, I returned to that old camp site searching for the band her captor's war party came from. Finally, that third summer I found their camp."

The old man removed a moccasin and began rubbing his exposed foot. When an owl hooted overhead, he hooted back.

"That one is content," the old man said, pointing his chin out into the gathering darkness, toward the hooting.

"What happened at the Blackfeet camp, Grandfather?" Lion Hunter prompted impatiently.

"That night I crept into their camp and stole meat from their drying racks to make friends with their dogs. I found my Pigeon's slave-lodge. She sat in the dirt outside a lodge, tied to a picket with a war pony who liked wild oats.

"Her body was much broken and weak. Her face was scarred as I have never before seen a face, but there was still anger in her, and she wanted to kill those who had made her a slave. I held her for a time so she would know she was with her family again. Then, I whispered to her that

I would go and prepare the hiding place we would need to make good her escape so she could plan her revenge. It was very hard to leave her side, but there was much to do before I could safely rescue her.

"The next night I returned and cut her free. We left the camp with a trail of many hungry dogs. But they went back when I gave no more meat to them. After we had passed the horse herds with their careless pasture boys, we moved quickly over paths the village used each day. We wore moccasins I stole from a Blackfeet warrior society lodge so they would not recognize the Crow pattern moccasins your mother made for me."

"Wait, Grandfather," Lion Hunter interrupted, stunned by the revelation. "My mother made your moccasins?"

"Yes. She also made this fine shirt for me. The Crow make fine clothes like our people make fine weapons. We are the same but different. We both make fine things."

"But why?" Lion Hunter was not just surprised that his mother would do such a thing—his heart flooded once again with hope that his mother might still be alive. "Is she still alive, Grandfather?"

"I cannot say. She could be with the Cloud People maybe, or our friends the Flat Heads. She journeyed south when last I saw her."

Lion Hunter, sitting up now, leaned forward, voice quivering. "Could we find her?"

"There will be time after you have become a warrior. This must come first. It is a promise I have made to my daughter so that she might fulfill her promise to your mother."

"Your daughter?" Lion Hunter echoed, stunned. "You have a daughter? Why does your daughter care that I become a warrior?" Both thoughts confused him.

"My daughter, your mentor, Kills-In-The-Dark. They are the same."

"Grandfather, these things are all new to me. My mother made you clothing before she left me with Kills-In-The-Dark? And Kills-In-The-Dark is your daughter?" Lion Hunter shook his head, holding it between both hands.

Spirit Man removed his second moccasin and, after wiggling his toes vigorously, began rubbing the foot. After a moment he looked up at Lion Hunter, waiting, but when the young brave asked no further questions, he shrugged and continued with his story.

"We traveled for a half of the night before we came to the place I prepared for our hiding. It was up a steep rock face where a vein of black rock had cracked and fallen away from the surrounding granite. The missing rock made a small hollow space big enough for both of us to crawl back into. Seep water pooled in a basin at its back before trickling out of sight through cracks in the floor. Nothing of it could be seen from the trail below.

"I brought some of the dried meat from the Blackfeet camp with us so we could stay hidden while the Blackfeet hunted us. During our wait, Pigeon was very brave. She never complained or became afraid. She sat and waited with the patience of a great heron standing still in the water waiting for its lunch. In that time, she told me the sad story of her captivity.

"In many night times of her slave life she was kept in a warrior society's lodge to be used by many warriors. In other times she was taken back to the lodge of two brothers, those who killed her family and captured her. The brothers' wives beat her with thorny switches often and cut off her nipples because she was young, and they did not want any babies their husbands made with her to live.

"She was weak from many wounds made upon her body by these mean wives and their husbands. When she tried to escape, they always found her because of her weakness and each new time they used their knives to carve more ugliness into her face and body. They did this to teach her, but she would not learn—always, she tried to escape again.

"My Pigeon spent three years as their captive and so she was seventeen when I stole her back, and we were once again together. She wanted to go back to kill the brothers and their wives. She also wanted to kill one other, a black-hearted warrior who was friend to the brothers—one who was crueler to her, she said, than all others. This one would return to the warrior lodge to humiliate her after all others had gone. He always tried to make her pretend she found joy in the things he did to her. When she would not, he became angry and tore at her wounds until she whimpered with pain."

Lion Hunter squirmed thinking about the pain young Pigeon must have suffered.

"She wanted to rest and eat for a few days, then return to make war on those who hurt her. I asked her to wait until I taught her the ways of the fox so she, like the fox, would know every shadow of her world and maybe find safety from her enemy. I was selfish—I knew she would not return to our people's village to live a long life if she hurried in her revenge-taking. She needed to learn how the animal-people of our world outlast their enemies to survive.

"After five days the Blackfeet gave up their search. So I scouted the next little way of our escape, and when I returned we moved to a new hiding place. Over the days that we sneaked back to our Wolf Ridge lands I taught her how to move in secret, like the fox, and to memorize the place of all hide-spots she found.

"She understood the good in my teaching and stayed with me learning for one year. My heart sang with the happiness of being beside my daughter each day. It was a time of great joy for this long dead father.

"Grandfather, did she learn to stalk as good as you?"

Spirit Man paused, and smiled.

"One day she went away to hunt." He absently made the signs for walk, then hunt. "When I went to the stream to get water my heart leaped in my chest, and Cold Maker of the north sent a river of ice through my body. My daughter, sitting in the shadows by the trailside, grabbed my ankle as I passed. Her eye shined with pleasure from my scare."

A quiet chuckle came from the now darkness-shadowed form of Spirit Man. Lion Hunter thought of the times the old man startled him in much the same way. He liked that Pigeon frightened Spirit Man. He thought it must have brought her great joy also.

"My daughter learned well. She studied the ways of all of the creatures around her but especially the ways of the fox, which is only seen when it wants to be seen. Pigeon made her own weapons, and she kept us rich with meat and herbs in that time. But, after that year, she again grew restless to seek her revenge.

"When summer brought her eighteenth year, my words could no longer hold her. So we returned to Blackfeet country, using our same hiding spots. She brought a fine stone war club made for her revenge and some moccasins she made in the Crow pattern like mine, those that your mother made.

"From her three slave years she knew where the Blackfeet band would camp. That first night, after we returned to the rock face hiding spot, she left to make ready for her revenge. After a time, I followed her. My heart hurt with worry that she would not return safely. But my daughter was not so reckless with excitement as are most young warriors.

"In her Crow moccasins, she first crept into the Blackfeet camp, stole some meat, and made sure her slave family still lived with this band. Then, she went to the place where the camp's women would go to make their gatherings the next day. The sun was not yet showing its face.

"In the morning, I found her and waited. She made a good hide there.

Lion Hunter interrupted. "Only two of you came for the revenge-taking?" With the whole Blackfeet band so near, their purpose seemed overwhelming to him.

Spirit Man stood, leaned back, and scratched his back against Grandmother's thick bark. After a moment's stretching he walked off into the surrounding forest, and the young brave heard him relieve himself. That was the only sound the old man made.

When he returned, Spirit Man sat down cross legged and scooped pine needles up around both sides of his skinny rump. He leaned to the right and pushed some of the debris beneath that cheek, then to the left and repeated his effort for the right.

"Hunter, we did not come to fight with the whole band, just those who hurt my Pigeon. Anyway, even the whole Wolf Ridge village would not be large enough to attack this one band of Blackfeet. Now, do you want to learn this story?"

"I am sorry, Grandfather. Please tell me her story."

"The Blackfeet women came to this valley, and she watched two of them—the mean wives, I thought. When these two were alone, she snuck up, clubbed the youngest in the head and then chased the fat one, who ran away screaming. But my Pigeon ran faster. She leaped on this woman's back and rode her into the ground. Then she sat on top of this fat woman and cut off her head even while she continued to resist. That frightened me."

"Grandfather, is this one of the heads that hang in her lodge now?" Lion Hunter was excited. He hadn't expected to learn about his mentor's trophies.

"Yes. And afterward, my Pigeon stood defiantly over the body, holding her trophy high overhead—screaming fiercely. In the old times, when I was alive and lived among my people, I went on many horse-stealing raids and on war parties too, but I never before saw such anger, and I never before saw an enemy's head cut from its body. This troubled me, but she was my daughter and I knew her pain was great from the three years of her slavery." Spirit Man bowed his head, picking absently at the fringe on his shirt.

"She then returned to the first woman and cut off her head also. After she was done she came straight to the place where I hid. I do not know how she knew I was there, but she held up her trophies for me to see. Your teacher, young Lion Hunter, is a skilled hunter and a dangerous warrior."

Spirit Man fell silent, shifting his position to find a more comfortable position.

When Spirit Man did not soon resume his story, Lion Hunter cleared his throat. "Grandfather, what happened next?" He was anxious to hear more, much more, about his mysterious mentor.

"I was fearful. I thought the whole Blackfeet nation would search forever until they found us because of the disrespect she made to these two wives. Then, I did not understand how well my daughter planned our escape.

"We trotted to the valley's creek where she washed the blood from her trophies, placed them in an herb bag she took from the second wife, and slung it over her shoulder.

"We stayed in the creek, trotting west away from the Blackfeet village. She led us to a rocky mountainside that came down to the water. We left the water there, carefully stepping our Crow moccasins on a few small dirt patches so those following would believe we traveled across the rocks hoping to fool their hunters and make our escape good.

After leaving this false trail, we returned to the creek and waded back the way we came, past the killing meadow to a place where the village path came up to the water's edge. Here, Pigeon pulled two pairs of Blackfeet moccasins from her carry pack and gave me a set. She told me to put them on before leaving the water.

"I was concerned about angry Blackfeet warriors coming upon us, so I quickly put them on while she changed hers. She put our Crow moccasins into the carry pack with her trophies.

"We soon came to the black-rock hide spot, but we did not stop to make camp and rest for two more days. The Blackfeet were maybe fooled by our false trail because we did not see any warriors for our whole journey back to Wolf Ridge land. My Pigeon's head-taking troubled me, but I was very proud of her fine raid."

Spirit Man, now a black shadow against the surrounding forest, leaned back against the Grandmother tree and rested in silence.

Hunter, his rapt attention suddenly pierced by the lack of the old man's gravelly voice, spoke up.

"But Grandfather, Kills-In-The-Dark has five heads hanging from her lodge pole, not two." Before the old man could answer, Lion Hunter erupted with another question, one that had played on the edges of his mind since the old man began his story.

"You said her family was taking her to the Red Rock band, but they were all killed. How can she be your daughter if those of her family were all killed here beneath Grandmother?"

After a long pause the old man responded, his tone sad.

"In the last year of my living time, when I was a fine warrior, I had a sweet wife. We were happy. I was a good provider, and Pigeon was growing in the softness of my wife's belly.

"In this time I led a raid to take ponies from the Crow. We were to be a group of seven warriors, but a Badger War Chief made a grand gift of five ponies to me in our warrior lodge two nights before the raid. I was surprised, but very proud, because he made big compliments to me in front of the other warriors.

"The next day, he came to me alone and asked if I remembered his gifts and asked me to take his son, Almost Tall, on my raid. This son was a new warrior who had already been awarded too many coups because his father was an important War Chief. I did not want to bring him along, but I had taken the chief's gifts and did not want to disrespect him, so I took Almost Tall on my raid.

"We stole six fine mares, including a beautiful spotted rump mare for my wife, and we were returning to our village when a terrible rainstorm came upon us. We hid under the hanging rock our people call the Trading Wall where Hidatsa traders camp each year with their pipestones, shells, rock bangles, and the many other things they trade. We were waiting out the storm when the rock wall crumbled down on us, killing all but Almost Tall and me. I was struck in the head by a falling rock, and both of my arms were broken. My thoughts were so wounded I could not think to travel, and I could not care for myself.

"Almost Tall stayed with me for a while, but when he saw a strange-looking skinny naked man approach on foot he became frightened. The strange one had two large ugly faces, one on the front of his head and another on the back. Both were painted with many bright colors. Almost Tall ran away and left me to die.

He told those of our village that all but him were killed in a fierce battle with many strange two-faced men, and, with his father's encouragement, he took both my lodge and my sweet wife as his own. I did not know these things until three moons later."

"Did you really see two-faced men?" Lion Hunter asked, eyes wide.

"The strange man was a wandering Dine medicine man who wore carved stick faces to frighten off evil spirits. I never met a Dine before, but I was interested when he told his desert stories during the many weeks he spent feeding me and chanting strange words over me to heal my wounds.

"He told me he was on a long-walk journey to the northeast where he heard fish traveled in great herds. I told him I saw the fish herds in my youth, and he would need a shirt to keep him warm in their country. He just nodded and laughed with the same funny little giggle he ended all of his talking. We both giggled when I told him his two faces had frightened off the make-believe warrior, Almost Tall.

"When I was healed and it was time to part, I gave him my war shirt so he would be warm in the land of the herding fish.

"The day I returned to my village I found Almost Tall with all that was mine, and I became crazy. I suffered the rage of a rutting bull buffalo. I charged into my lodge and hit Almost Tall with my war club. Then I threw him out of the teepee so I could be alone with my wife.

"He ran away just as he had at the rockslide, but this time, he returned with his father, the War Chief. Both began yelling outside of my teepee. They said I was violating Almost Tall's lodge and threatened to have the camp-police warriors beat me and force me from the village. When I came outside, the make-believe warrior stood behind his father and a large crowd of our people.

"I was still angry at the chief because he tricked me into taking his coward son on my raid. So I hit him with my war club and knocked him down and his cowardly son ran away again, whimpering like a stepped-on dog.

"There is more to this story, but at its end I was banished. I was dead to my people. In the time of a mosquito's life I had no more people, no more family—I was banished from my people's village and I would be dead to them forever.

"The coward warrior was too frightened to take my wife again. I met secretly with my best friend, who was your blood grandfather. He took my pregnant wife into his lodge to care for. He became my wife's husband and, when my Pigeon was born, he became her father because he was not dead like me.

"Then, in my Pigeon's fourteenth year, he took his wife, who before was my wife, and my daughter, on a journey to find husbands for them.

"Your grandfather's two sons, both already warriors and married, did not go on this journey with him.

"So the father killed here under this tree, by the Blackfeet, was your grandfather, my best friend.

"I am tired now, we will sleep, and in the morning, I will tell you of the long-night-stalk that changed my daughter's name. Then we will return your pony to the

Wolf Ridge camp and go away to learn more of the rest of the world."

8

The sun's face peeked over the eastern horizon laying soft light down over the tips of the Grandmother tree's upper-most branches. Lion Hunter, leaning back against her thick trunk, took in the soft music of the morning breeze as it wafted through the pine forest's swaying needles.

The morning insects awaken. I will get firewood after I listen for a while.

It was a welcome change living apart from his people, away from the constant commotion of their gossip and banter, the noise of camp chores, and the chaos of capering children. Lion Hunter looked forward to his upcoming vision quest—to the quiet time he would spend alone, waiting for the spirit world's personal message to him—for the vision that he hoped would reveal the purpose of his life.

Spirit Man, resting nearby, opened his eyes, briefly scanned his surroundings then looked across at Lion Hunter. He smiled, pulled his bony legs close and rose, all without perceptible sound. Lion Hunter watched as Sprit Man walked off into the forest, consciously listening for any noise. He heard only the wake-up sounds of the insects.

Lion Hunter didn't know how old Spirit Man was. Kills-In-The-Dark and Lion Hunter's father were the only two adults who ever spoke of the old man to Lion Hunter, and neither mentioned his age.

How can an old man be so noiseless?

Assuming Spirit Man walked off to relieve himself, Lion Hunter waited, enjoying his quiet time.

"The fox moves only when the attention of those around it have journeyed elsewhere."

Lion Hunter leaped to his feet and spun, facing the direction of the startling words.

"Why do you always do this thing, Grandfather? It is not a fun game."

"Only by knowing what is happening all around you can you hope to survive. Tell me, do you smell horsemint, almost-warrior? I have rubbed its smell upon my hands and arms."

"I smell it," Lion Hunter spat back, silently admitting to himself his senses had been wandering—something a real warrior should not do. He was still churning when Spirit Man began speaking again.

"My Pigeon and her family were camped here. I think their killers maybe surprised them by coming from this same direction," said the old man. "Look, the brambles seem very thick here, but there are narrow patches of moss in the dampness behind these bushes—the Blackfeet could have used this place to quietly sneak up on her family. The old man looked toward the base of Grandmother, as though deciding if he wanted to sit there, as he had the night before."

I see only where you snuck up on me. I think you must have tricked me into lying here last night.

Lion Hunter tried to remember if the old man did anything to encourage his selection of the particular sleeping place he used last night but he could not. He clenched his teeth, pushing away the frustration of again failing to detect the old man's approach.

"It is something to remember, I think," Spirit Man suggested gently, "and do not be angry with this old dead man who has only gladness in his heart for you. Come, sit and I will tell you the rest of my Pigeon's name-change story.

Spirit Man pressed his hand to Lion Hunter's shoulder as he passed walking toward the bed of pine needles he'd scraped together for last night's sleep. Before sitting, he reached behind his back and tried to scratch its middle but soon gave up with a sigh. Still chafed, Lion Hunter found brief satisfaction in the old man's failure.

Lion Hunter dropped down and leaned his own back against the Grandmother tree. He felt an odd sensation trickle down his backbone and wondered if Grandmother might be sending him strength from the spirit world, or…

Maybe it is only ants, mad at me for disturbing them. He twisted around and inspected the tree's bark attempting to scratch, as had Grandfather, at his back. There were no ants.

Eyes closed, he imagined himself far away, wandering a vast plain of gently swaying grasses. His nerves were calmed by the time Spirit Man spoke again.

"It is as you said last night," Spirit Man began. "My daughter keeps five head-trophies in her lodge, not two."

Lion Hunter opened his eyes, wearily focusing on the old man. He would listen to his words, but he would also carefully sample the surrounding breezes for new smells. He did not want to make the mistake of inattention again.

"The first two heads are those of the two Blackfeet wives whose story I have already told you. The others are of those who killed her family and kept her as a slave for three years, and a black-spirit warrior who made my Pigeon beg for her life too many times. I will tell you the story of these three now."

Spirit Man glanced around the needle-littered earth that surrounded him. His eyes lit up as he reached out and fished a thick twig from the debris. He began scratching at his back before speaking, his face soft with pleasure.

"My Pigeon and I," he finally began, "stayed away from Blackfeet lands for three moons after the wife killings. After that, she would wait no longer. So again, we left the safety of our own homelands and went to avenge her slave years. My daughter brought the two wife-heads with us on this journey. I would not help her carry them because I feared the Grandfather Spirits would not like the strangeness of that behavior. She carried them in a pack. This was not a great burden for her because they were not so heavy as when she first took them. In our waiting time, she emptied them of their meats and their skins were dried and shriveled from hanging in the smoke of many campfires so that there were no more juices in them. They were terrible to look at. Then, I did not understand why she brought them with us on the rest of her revenge-taking journey."

Lion Hunter imagined how bulky her carry-pack must have been. It was truly a strange thing to do. He shrugged his shoulders, then leaned forward and scratched his back again—Kills-In-The-Dark was strange, everyone knew that.

"Once we found the new Blackfeet camp, we hid nearby, watching their comings and goings for many days. We took much food from their camp in this time, even two elk skins, and we became good friends with their mangy dogs who came sometimes to eat with us. Because of our thefts, we often heard quarrelling between lodge neighbors while we hid near the fields where women gathered wood and herbs." Lifting his eyes to the sky, the old man chuckled.

Lion Hunter also laughed, imagining how such thievery might disrupt the peace of his own village if his people believed their neighbors were stealing from them. Thinking about his village and his people brought the soft-eyed image of Willow to his mind. He quickly glanced up.

Did you see my thoughts, old man?

Spirit Man's eyes were gazing out over the distant plain.

"One day, we saw three warriors ride away from the Blackfeet camp," Spirit Man resumed. "They led a string of five extra ponies, one with many furs lashed to its back. My Pigeon laughed when she saw them. It was an uncaring laugh.

"She told me, 'the tall one is mean—he is the always-angry brother. That small brown pony was my mother's for riding before her death. The always-angry brother took it and made me ride it after his war party killed my family.

Now, he takes these skins and five extra ponies away from his village. They are all his, I remember. I think he journeys to another village to get a new wife. The others come with him so he will not be robbed of his furs and ponies. They are gifts, maybe—gifts for the father of a new wife.'

"She also told me, 'the one who sits on his pony bent to one side is his brother. I think he cannot get a new wife now because he broke his back when he fell from a horse during a hunt after I was his slave. Others in the village now leave food for him—there is no pride left in his lodge. That third warrior is the black-spirit of my sleep terrors. My hate for him is greatest of all.'"

Lion Hunter removed two strips of jerky from the elk pack, holding one out to Spirit Man as he took a bite from the other. He dropped the extra piece in his lap when the old man shook his head to the offer.

Spirit Man continued, "We waited until night to sneak into the Blackfeet herd and steal two ponies so we could follow the two brothers and their friend. It was easy—the pasture boys were very lazy."

"Grandfather, were they the same pasture boys as when you snuck through the herd before the wife-killings?" Lion Hunter asked around a mouthful of jerky.

"I do not know, but I think it does not matter. When you were a pasture boy for your father's herd, did you ever sleep or play games with your friends?"

Lion Hunter looked away, remembering how quickly the thrill of being allowed to care for his father's herd wore off and boredom set in. Spirit Man stretched a leg out and nudged Lion Hunter's foot with his own. Lion Hunter looked back finding a warm smile on the old man's face. Reassured, he smiled back.

"Our own Wolf Ridge warriors," Spirit Man continued, "make raids to steal ponies guarded by Crow boys no more than ten winters old, and these warriors always make big congratulations to themselves for being so brave. They are maybe not so courageous. Young braves are only boys busy dreaming of being warriors. I think maybe they dream too much and are not good herd watchers. What do you think, Lion Hunter?"

Lion Hunter saw the twinkle in Spirit Man eyes and looked away again, blushing.

"Well, my Pigeon and I rode for three days, staying far behind these riders so we would not be discovered.

"My Pigeon found no joy in our stalking—she was a fox, thinking only of the perfect time for her revenge-taking. I was fearful of the danger to both of us, but it was the first time this dead man had ridden a pony for many years, and I was filled with a great pleasure that rubbed out much of my worry. Danger and pleasure are strange brothers."

The old man paused, looking out over the plain. He smiled oddly, as though he too might blush, but a moment later he lifted his chin, squared his old shoulders, and cleared his throat. He continued.

"On the third night, we hobbled our ponies in a small wash with steep rock walls on three sides and crept up near to the stand of cottonwood trees where the three Blackfeet made their sleep-camp. We waited and watched until all slept. I rubbed oats on me, like the horsemint from before."

His sideways glance momentarily renewed a sense of embarrassment in Lion Hunter.

"I slipped up to their ponies and fed each a handful of oats, then sat with them. Once they had become my friends, I untied the hobbles from their legs. I knew they would follow me when I crept away. They hoped for more oats, and I gave them enough to make sure they were far away from the camp before I stopped giving it to them.

"It was a big moon that night. So I hid in tree shadows watching as my daughter fox-sneaked into their camp. She set one wife-head next to each of the two brothers. She also took all of the warrior's lances and bows, and we left. She is a very good fox, I think."

Lion Hunter nodded, remembering the many times he watched her approaching unsuspecting animals during hunts.

"Later, after the moon set and while it was still very dark, we went to find the Blackfeet ponies. Because they remained close together, we gathered them easily, and the warriors could not hear because the sounds of a creek between their camp and us covered our noise.

"In that time, I felt like a warrior again and excitement filled my chest. It was a fine feeling."

Lion Hunter watched the old man's smile-wrinkles bunch up and felt the excitement of his words beginning to bunch his muscles. The hair on the back of his neck felt prickly.

"We took the stolen ponies to our end-canyon and tied all together except a brown-and-white paint. That one was the angry-brother's favorite and why my Pigeon chose to ride it to her revenge taking.

"Like all Wolf Ridge warriors preparing for war, my Pigeon stripped herself of all clothing except her loincloth then grabbed up her weapons and rode off toward the Blackfeet camp. She rode and I walked, both in silence. Looking from the corners of my eyes I saw the many angry moonlight shadows that were her scars from captivity. The strange patterns of those mutilations made a great hurt in my heart for all her pain and for the stone face she hid that pain behind."

Lion Hunter understood—he saw her many scars and often thought of how painful receiving them must have been.

"She slung her bow and arrows across her shoulders, then slipped the loop of the heavy war club over her wrist as she muttered words beneath her breath. I think maybe she spoke in the Blackfeet tongue.

"It was still dark and just before daylight when we reached the top of the creek's bank across from their camp. My Pigeon stopped her muttering long enough to tell me she would make her war with the Blackfeet alone. I was fearful for her safety, but I was relieved. The years of my exile have made me very careful. In those years I mostly showed myself only to friends so that I would not be killed." The old man chuckled. "A dead man being killed is strange to think about. Do not be made dead by your people, Hunter. It twists your thoughts."

Lion Hunter fidgeted, waiting for the exciting part of Spirit Man's story.

"What happened then, Grandfather?" he urged.

"The creek was not deep—a pony's hoof, maybe, no more, and only a stone's throw wide. The Blackfeet camp was another stone's throw from the other side.

"My Pigeon sat the angry-brother's paint with the war club dangling from her wrist and bow and arrows slung across her back. The Blackfeet had only their knives and would be on foot. So I sat down in the night shadow of a white pine to watch and hope.

"My daughter started down the steep creek bank taking no care for the noise the pony made. I grew more afraid for her with each of its loud steps. At the time I did not know how foolish my fear was. I was just an old dead man—I did not yet know the war-spirit that was inside my Pigeon's heart.

"The pony's hooves clacked loudly against the rocks in the clay bank, sounds that knifed through the morning silence. She rode down so slowly I feared the Blackfeet might be up and upon her before she even reached the bottom. But her enemies were too busy for that.

"Bits of pink light showed on the surrounding hilltops as the sun began its wakeup but at the bottom of the bank, where my Pigeon and her pony now waited, all was still black shadow.

"In the warrior camp I saw three dim shadows not yet fully colored by the morning light. They scurried this way and that like stirred-up ants—looking for their weapons, I think. When they could not find them, their concern grew and their faces returned to my Pigeon's black shadow more and more often, each time with greater alarm.

"The tallest shadow in their camp, the always-angry brother, made a sudden cry and pitched over backward, falling to the ground on his backside. He leapt back to his feet immediately and crabbed forward to the gray lump he had fallen away from. His grey shadow hunched over, staring down at this thing on the ground, and the others, interrupting their frightened searches, turned to stare with him. Light was growing in the east.

"Silence stretched for many breaths before his shadow arched back and bellowed out a great howl so loud that even brave enemies might think to run away in fear. But through this all my Pigeon sat in the black shadow of the bank on her side of the creek, watching, her silence so loud no single bird thought to make its song. She was a lethal predator at the end of its stalking, and these three Blackfeet warriors now knew… they were being hunted by the black shadow of death.

"Slowly, the always-angry brother turned, standing to his full height to face the threat that lurked in the shadow beyond the creek. The others stood also, and in that time I felt a terrible ending coming, but I knew I should fear no more for my daughter. My fear was for the violence and cruelty of what was to come.

"The morning's light grew bolder and the Blackfeet warriors watched as the menacing shadow grew visible, and they saw only a woman—a slave woman they all knew, sitting on the angry-brother's favorite pony. The warrior in them returned.

"But I think you are maybe not interested in hearing the rest of this story. You already know she has cut off their heads."

"No, Grandfather! I want to hear," Lion Hunter blurted. "Tell me, please."

9

"Well, then," Spirit Man said, and cleared his throat. He intentionally prolonged the tense moment while peeking over at Lion Hunter to measure his excitement. He tilted his head back as though having to think back to where he left off in his storytelling before continuing.

"Below my sitting place under the white pine, all four stood very still—the three Blackfeet warriors in their camp and my Pigeon sitting upon the always-angry brother's pony on my side of the creek. There was no sound, not even the tiniest breeze, and a chill settled over my father's-heart. Once more I doubted the outcome of this war. I was so tense—I jumped when the always-angry brother took his first stride toward my daughter. He had only a knife but there was fury in his walk. I think in that moment he did not see a threat—he saw only that a woman mocked him. Soon, he walked faster, his face hard with his anger.

"Still my Pigeon did not move. Only after he crossed much of the way between them did she calmly turn *his* war-pony and guide it along the shallow edge of the water—away from the always-angry brother's advance. There were no sounds in the quiet morning except the soft sounds of her pony's footsteps in the water."

Spirit Man's eyes met with Lion Hunter's. He squinted and hunched forward in a hunting predator's posture.

"Like the wolf cutting off a deer, his walk became a trot on a line to meet the end of this new path she took. Maybe he told those others not to join in his killing—I do not know. But they stayed in the camp, watching while he came for her. His courage was foolish. He would soon need help, and the other warriors would be too far away.

"When the pony broke into a water-splashing lope, the warrior erupted into an excited sprint, whooping triumphantly, running faster to intercept his slave woman. Maybe he believed she was fleeing.

"My daughter, the warrior, did not glance his way or give him a chance to tire. She wheeled the paint around, kicking her heels into the pony's ribs while giving it full rein. The powerful pony stretched out, pounding through the shallow water, racing toward the Blackfeet. The always-angry brother would not change his path and so each ran toward the other. Maybe the Blackfeet thought my Pigeon would turn to the side at the last moment so she could attack him with her war club. Or maybe he did not think. I do not know. But she did not turn, and he did not turn.

"The paint crashed into the Blackfeet, pitching him over and over in the water beneath its churning legs. By the time my daughter slowed the pony and turned it back, the Blackfeet struggled back to a sitting position and sat there staring down at his twisted legs. The creek's water swirled around him. He braced himself back on his arms, holding himself up in that position. But his head had no more sense in it, I think."

"Did the other Blackfeet come then?" Lion Hunter leaned forward, poking at Spirit Man's knee.

Spirit Man smiled at him.

"Not yet. Do you want me to continue or do you only want to ask questions?"

"Please, Grandfather, do not stop."

"Let's see, where was I?"

"Grandfather!"

"Okay then. My Pigeon made a war-glare back at the other two Blackfeet as she pulled to a stop and threw her leg over the paint's withers to slide down in front of the trampled warrior. As soon as her feet splashed into the water she attacked, her war club smashing his face again and again until he fell back into the hoof-deep water, blood swirling in the current around him.

"Breaths later she stood to her full height and, with her war club dangling from her wrist, looked back at the two shocked warriors standing at the edge of their camp. Her eyes still on them, she drew her knife, sat down on the dead warrior's chest, and plunged the blade into his neck.

The two remaining warriors sprinted toward her, screaming out their war cries. But they started too late.

"My Pigeon grabbed the dead man's hair, forcing his head back and, pulling her blade free, sliced into the meat of his neck. But the two warriors were coming.

"I worried about her calm, thinking she could not finish and remount her pony soon enough. The broke-back brother was falling behind, but the black-spirit warrior came fast.

"It is not so easy to part a head from its body. We all know this from dressing out our kills. When my Pigeon finally sat up from this work, she coolly splashed her knife in the water to clean the blood from it. This took so much time I began to fear for her life. But I worried alone.

"The black-spirit warrior, he who was the ghost of my Pigeon's night terrors, ran with the speed of a deer. He thought to gain advantage by seizing the nervous paint, I think.

"My Pigeon stood up and sheathed her knife—watching the black-spirit who grew nearer with each breath. My heart was filled with fear but, finally, she grabbed the pony's mane, made one last glare, then swung up onto the pony's back. The frost of Cold Maker's north winds was in her warrior's heart.

"At the last moment she kicked the pony's sides so hard I heard the hollow sound from where I sat. The paint lurched to full speed, pounding toward the black-spirit but he was wily. In the last breath, he dove to the side away from my Pigeon's war club. When she passed, he quickly scrambled back to his feet, but he could only watch as she left him far behind—speeding toward the limping form of the broke-back brother.

"The black-spirit warrior was brave, and smart, but I think now he knew my Pigeon was smart too, and that she would soon come back for him.

"The broke-back brother, now running away from her, fell beneath my Pigeon's club, backbone crushed. I heard this terrible sound, and watched as his body fell limp. He began bawling like a lost buffalo calf.

"My Pigeon let the paint, her pony now, slow to a walk. She calmly circled back, ignoring the broke-back brother's wails and eased toward the black-spirit warrior who was now midway between creek and camp. As long as she was on her pony and he was on foot in the open, she had the advantage. I knew that, my Pigeon knew that, and the black-spirit knew that.

"My heart felt great joy for this day as the sun's ball broke fully from the distant hill and all shadows fled from their battlefield. Fierce hatred filled the faces of these two enemies—the slave-torturer and the revenge-taker.

"Her enemy watched her hard, angling his walk, hoping to reach the safety of the trees while the broke-back brother continued his bawling, a shameless plea for mercy made to a morning without kindness.

"But the black-spirit warrior would not run. I think he did not want to shame himself. It was a proud warrior's mistake.

"Still walking her pony, my Pigeon moved into his path with calculated ease. Each time he turned, she turned, always remaining between the black-spirit and the safety of the trees—glaring down at him from the pony's back.

"When he walked faster, she urged the paint to move at this new speed and so they continued, turning and moving and turning again. Finally, he stopped and stood facing her, chin lifted, arms crossed over his chest. He knew he could not reach the trees.

"He did not see my Pigeon as a woman to torture anymore, I think." Spirit Man chuckled and Lion Hunter, his breath shallow, squirmed, waiting for more.

"He saw death, I think." Spirit Man's face broke into a broad smile. "His warrior's heart remained, but I am sure it no longer beat with the sureness it felt all those nights in the warrior society's lodge when he was hurting her.

"My Pigeon stopped the paint in front of the black-spirit—just far enough away to tempt him to rush across the distance and attack her. She sat silent—her face cold and hard.

"The black-spirit was already dead, but I knew he would not quit.

"When he did not attack, she yanked the pony's reins back-heeling its ribs at the same time. The pony kicked and scuffed at the earth in confusion. It danced in a circle around the black-spirit as she sat straight-backed, glaring down at him.

"At first the Blackfeet turned with her, looking his defiance back at her. But then, I think, he became embarrassed again and he quit turning always to face her. He set his jaw and stood looking off at the too-far-away trees. She tightened her challenging circle, still trying to tempt him into attack. When at last he did, the pony lurched away so quickly the warrior bounced off of its flank and fell to his knees.

"He scrambled back to his feet and again crossed his arms and stared away. He stood, and she circled. No warrior's honor was in their battle—there was only the black-spirit's arrogant hatred and my Pigeon's cold revenge-taking. I think maybe the Spirit Fathers will not praise this war-making when these two journey to the world beyond. It was too ugly, without the nobility of warriors who fight to protect their people. But she was still my Pigeon and the sufferings of her night visions were wounds that, I feared, would not otherwise heal. I wished for her to kill this Blackfeet warrior. There was no care in my heart for his suffering, but I wished for the poison in her heart to be released."

The old man's expression was sad as he gazed far out onto the plain. He took a deep breath and let the cool air cleanse his thoughts.

"When he could not be tempted into a second attack," Spirit Man resumed, still looking off in the distance, "my Pigeon made a wider circle, continuing until she was behind him. There, she suddenly kicked the paint into another earth-pounding charge, and, again, he dived to the side, barely escaping her attack. After she passed, he quickly leaped back to his feet, this time looking all around him for some advantage, but there was none. This warrior was already dead but he would not die just because she wanted him to.

"The black-spirit stood only a moment longer, then abruptly sat down cross legged and looked away, again toward the trees. He was a proud warrior. Each time my Pigeon stopped before him, he turned his head to a different direction. It was a stubborn time for them both. Finally, after a long stare, my Pigeon pulled the bow loose from her shoulder and notched an arrow. Without pause she drew back the arrow and shot him in the belly.

"The Blackfeet jolted when the bolt pierced him. He first looked down at the protruding shaft, then up at my Pigeon, his expression stunned. When, after that moment, he looked back down it was to scan the ground around him.

"Finding a rock, he reached out and picked it up. His body winced with the movement, but beyond that he refused to show pain. He set the rock between his legs and immediately gripped the protruding shaft with both hands and broke off its feathered end. He grabbed the rock up again and struck at the broken end of the arrow until its point broke through the skin of his back.

"Broke-back's far-away bawling continued, while the black-spirit clenched his jaw, locked eyes with my Pigeon, and silently reached around behind his back and yanked the bloody shaft from his body.

"All hunters know, an arrow in the belly kills. Slowly, but it kills. And it kills painfully. This black-spirit warrior would not admit this. He rose and stood staring at her for another long time. Then, looking away, he suddenly began sprinting toward the trees. She wheeled the paint but yanked away hard when the black-spirit suddenly leaped sideways at her. As she passed, he grabbed the pony's tail. The animal panicked, lurching from side to side, nearly unseating my Pigeon as she dug her heels in and slapped back at the warrior's arms with her bow. But he held onto the tail, barely keeping his feet, again and again struggling to climb up over the bucking animal's rump to get at my daughter.

"All was a confusing whirl, like the great spinning winds that come to our plains in the summer. Thick dust kicked up around them, and the black-spirit yipped out long war cries as he continued his attack. Pigeon threw her bow aside, hefted her war club, and deliberately wrenched the paint sideways in a wheeling turn, into the struggling warrior's attack.

"Her first blow smashed down into his exposed shoulder. Immediately she made the paint wheel in the opposite direction and landed a second blow to the other shoulder. Again and again she did this, until his hands fell away from the pony. She continued to spin furiously, again and again striking at his shoulders as he staggered around trying to remain on his feet. With his neck stretched out and body leaning toward her, the Blackfeet ignored the blows she rained down on him. No longer able to attack, he looked his defiance back up into her eyes.

"Then her attack was over. The black-spirit still stood, the bones in his shoulders so badly crushed they sagged against his chest, arms useless. Still, he looked.

"All three stood winded—the pony and two warriors, their chests heaving in the chill morning air, breath-clouds spraying from the flared nostrils of all.

"In the quiet I heard the broke-back brother again, now sobbing, his Blackfeet words shamelessly making the sounds of a beggar.

"Pigeon glanced once in his direction but returned her attention to the black-spirit. She threw her leg over the pony's withers and again slid off the animal's shoulder. She landed facing the black-spirit. There was no kindness in her for her defeated enemy. She cocked her head to the side, studied him for a moment, then walked around him.

"When she returned to his front, the warrior stretched up to his full height, leaned into her face, and let out a great defiant scream. She stood listening to that scream until it died away.

"Without expression, she unsheathed her knife and stepped close enough to rest its tip between the ribs of his heaving chest. He stood straight and again locked eyes with her.

"He said something to her in his Blackfeet language and smiled cruelly, but she did not speak back to him. Without expression, she pushed the knife into his heart and let him fall away from it."

"What did he say to her, Grandfather?"

"I think he said he was glad he made her so ugly."

10

"She took the heads of the always-angry brother and the black-spirit warrior without further ritual, then rode toward the Blackfeet camp to reclaim the two women's heads. Out on the field, the broke-back brother continued to weep. Finally, she rode back to him and dismounted. Because his body could not move, he lay on his back. But he turned his head, keeping her in sight while he begged like a baby bird. She set three of the heads on the ground before him. His wife's, she held back. The morning grew so quiet I could hear the soft noise of the insect nation's daytime talk.

"My Pigeon sat down on the ground before him. I could hear her speak the Blackfeet words, but she never told me what she said to this broke-back warrior.

"There was fear in his face when she later stood and held out his wife's head. Fear turned to terror when she set the gruesome trophy down on his chest, its empty eye sockets staring down at him. He sobbed, pleaded for her to finish him, to kill him.

"She did."

* * *

"Afterward, we let all of their ponies go so that we could not be followed on our journey home. My Pigeon was silent for three moons during our journey. Then, she stopped one day and looked at me with such sorrow I wanted to hold her to my chest, to protect her forever. But I knew she could not allow this.

"She told me, 'The Black Feet made an ugliness inside of me. There is no joy in my heart for their killing, only the relief of knowing these three men and the two wives are no more. I am changed. I am a warrior now. I can never be a woman again. I will be called Kills-In-The-Dark from this day forever.'

"I was sad because I lost my Pigeon that day, but she was Kills-In-The-Dark the warrior now, and the father in me felt much pride for her.

"One day, before we came to the Wolf Ridge village, she touched my arm, so unsure it almost could not be. 'I thank you, Father,' she said and my heart sang with the joy of a thousand new mornings. In our long time together she had never called me by that name or any other."

"But Grandfather, she did not kill the Blackfeet in the dark. Why did she take this name?"

Spirit Man paused, cocking his head to the side and studying Lion Hunter for long moments before he responded.

"The darkness was in her heart, Lion Hunter."

* * *

"When we came to the hills near our people's village," Spirit Man again took up his story, "I waited until I saw your father leave on a hunt. We went to him to ask for his help. I told him my Pigeon's story, and I asked him to take her back to the village so she could be with her people. I think you know the rest of her tale, Lion Hunter."

His story complete, Spirit Man sat quiet watching Lion Hunter reflect on the long tale. The sun was high now and flies pestered Black Storm, who stood swishing his tail and vigorously twitching his skin.

Lion Hunter gazed off into the distance. Finally, shading his eyes from the slanting rays of the afternoon sun, he looked back at the old man.

"Grandfather, was Kills-In-The-Dark's naming-story a lesson for my vision quest?"

Spirit Man shifted his eyes so he, too, looked out over the rolling plains. He took up a nearby twig, absently scratching in the dirt for long moments before he responded.

"Tell me, young Lion Hunter, do you remember the wolf leader, the Big Black?"

"Yes."

"He was a mighty leader, was he not?"

"I think yes, Grandfather. Many of his tribe followed him into battle."

"And yet, four of his tribe were killed because of his choice," Spirit Man paused, tossing the stick aside before looking up to continue.

"The heart has two sides, Lion Hunter, one that feels and one that sees. I think the Big Black used only the feel side of his heart when he made his choice to kill the she-bear's young for killing his mate and young pups. His heart did not *see* the many before-times when the mother bear avoided the wolf family's den, and he also did not *see* the sadness of all the tomorrow-times when he would miss those four of his family who were killed in the attack. His heart could *feel* only the terrible sadness and anger of his now time. I think it is maybe better to feel *and* to see than … to just feel or just see.

"You know the choices Carries-His-Lion makes," the old man continued. "He uses only the feel side of his heart. For him there is no before-time or tomorrow-time. His decisions are made always in the now-time because his heart is blinded by its feelings. Camp Chief Weasel Bear is different—his heart sees always our people's tomorrow-time. It is why our people seek his counsel for important choices they will make in their tomorrow-times. Do you understand these things, Lion Hunter?"

Lion Hunter delayed his response, more imitating his mentor's habit of thoughtfulness than true deliberation. Eventually though, he nodded, squinting back at the old man sitting across from him.

Spirit Man asked, "When Kills-In-The-Dark made her revenge choices, what side of her heart did she use, Lion Hunter?"

"The feel side. I think she did not want to see her before-time and maybe did not care about her tomorrow-time."

"Yes, I think so. My Pigeon's choices can be as cunning as the coyote's but all in her world is suffering. Do you see how this makes her heart blind to joy, Lion Hunter?"

"Yes," Lion Hunter responded, thinking how important this strange blindness must be to her.

"When a warrior makes choices that touch the lives of others, it is maybe best not only to feel their today-sufferings but also to see their tomorrow-joys. It is a thing to consider."

The old man sat quietly, allowing Lion Hunter to ponder what he had just been told before adding a final thought.

"A leader understands these things. You will be a leader one day, I think. When you understand what part of the heart a man makes his choice with, you can speak to the side that will hear you."

11

The weather turned after their arrival at the Grandmother Tree. It was hot now, even this high on the mountain. Below, out of the forest, on the rolling grass and sage-covered floor of the river basin, it would be scorching. Spirit Man and Lion Hunter, who led Black Storm, walked down and through the sweet-smelling pine forest and settled into the shadows near the edge of the mountain's lowest trees. They would start their journey in the early evening after the winds quieted, wanting to take advantage of the half-moon's light and cooler hours of darkness.

Lion Hunter sat and gazed down over the sweltering basin. He focused on one of several columns of rising dust, watching as it danced erratically for a few brief moments then dissolved. Others took its place as the winds below continued their buffeting journey westward along the floor of the Wind River valley. Dust devils were common in late summer, especially in the early evening when dry desert winds gusted up through gaps in the Rattle Snake Mountains that stood black on the basin's southern horizon. The frantic intensity of the winds would diminish as the sun disappeared behind the massive rock barrier of the Wind Mountains westward and the Rockies beyond. That was the path direction he and the old man would be traveling.

* * *

It took two days for Lion Hunter and Spirit Man to find the most recent Wolf Ridge village site. His people were camped on the sprawling river plain near the banks of a bend long ago cut off from the mother river by a rockslide. The floor of the cutoff was now a lush meadow and provided good graze for Wolf Ridge herds.

The two travelers sat atop a rise in the valley floor, plotting Lion Hunter's approach. Spirit Man would conceal himself while Lion Hunter returned Black Storm to Kills-In-The-Dark's herd, and they would continue their wilderness journey on foot. From where they were, the camp lodges were barely as tall as a hand held out at the end of an arm.

They had traveled all night, and it was late morning, the time of day when the faint morning breezes tapered off. He was downwind from the village. Even from this distance, Lion Hunter could smell the distinctive scent of the pony herds. Black Storm nickered—ears pricked and eyes bright with the expectation of seeing friends.

Leaving the old man sitting on a rock outcropping, Lion Hunter waved, and then rode off toward the village. Once down on the cutoff's grassy floor, he savored the feeling of a cool air current wafting over his bare torso. It was nearly noon, and the temperature was already rising. He rounded the last turn in the channel and was already into the fringes of the herd before the alerting ponies caught a pasture boy's attention. Pasture boys, mostly nine, ten, or eleven-year-olds, were notorious for becoming distracted from their duties.

No wonder our enemies travel so far to steal our ponies.

Lion Hunter, nearly sixteen, scowled down at one of the pasture boys in stone-faced silence as he passed.

At first, the boy looked away, but he was unable to contain his exuberance and quickly changed tactics by grabbing a handful of the closest pony's mane and swinging himself up to the animal's back, where he whooped and kicked the animal into action. He was already near the center of the herd before he'd settled himself on the pony's back.

Yes, go tell the other boys how you discovered me before I reached the herd. Lion Hunter smirked.

Lion Hunter spotted the handful of ponies Kills-In-The-Dark owned. Bunched together, all lifted their heads, anticipating being reunited with their herd mate. He rode up to them and dropped off the black pony's shoulder. They eagerly greeted him, sniffing and making soft sounds.

Lion Hunter shooed one away just to get the black's halter off and set him free.

Go, Black Storm. Find joy in the welcoming nickers of your kind.

Most young males worked as pasture boys with the village herd. If a boy's father owned one or more horses, the son's duties were to watch and safeguard his property. If a boy's father had no horses, he might volunteer to watch the horses of a warrior with a daring reputation for bravery, basking in the shadow of that warrior's deeds. Pasture boys endlessly rode the horses they were in charge of, pretending to be warriors themselves. They learned every peculiarity and ability of each horse and, more often than not, knew more about the animal than its true owner.

Of course, Kills-In-The-Dark had no one to watch her ponies. Village boys that age believed she was a witch, or at least were so frightened of her hideous appearance they made it a point to stay away from anything that had to do with her. So, the dominant mare of the group herded the medicine woman's horses apart from the rest, and they were usually found on the fringes of the village herd where there was better graze. After being released, Black Storm would remain nearby so the group was protected from predators. Looking over the tiny herd, Lion Hunter smiled. No other woman in their village owned a string of horses.

She owns ponies just like male warriors—more than some of the less fortunate warriors. Yet another reason for them to dislike her.

Back at the Grandmother Tree, when Spirit Man told him they were returning to the village, Lion Hunter's mind had immediately turned to Willow. He remembered the young maiden's pretty round face and long black hair laced into a single braid that she let hang down the front of her plain, buckskin dress. Now, as he drew near the village, he obsessed over the soft smile and fleeting eye contact with which she always greeted him. Lion Hunter resolved to catch a glimpse of her while walking through the Wolf Ridge campsite.

He knew that Willow's family usually raised their lodge near the village center, close to Chief Weasel Bear, who was her father's close friend. Lion Hunter approached the lodges but could not yet see the bright red ponies her father painted on the outside of his teepee. He did see a large black and yellow bear painted on a nearby teepee. That was Weasel Bear's lodge.

Lion Hunter walked among the village lodges with squared shoulders, intending to strut his way through the middle of camp.

If she is doing chores outside her father's lodge, she will see a fine almost-warrior.

Head facing straight forward and eyes straining at their sides, he fretted over how he might most attractively carry his body. He considered lifting his chin a little more or draping his forearm over the butt of his casually shouldered lance. In the end, though, he left the lance dangling at arm's length. He chose instead to reach his other arm back over his shoulder and grip the limb of his hunting bow, which, along with his quiver, was slung crosswise over his torso. He imagined the taut muscles of his forearm bulging handsomely.

There were no villagers in sight. Most escaped the heat by napping inside their teepees with the bottom skins rolled up, allowing chance small breezes to pass through. Village dogs, sprawled in whatever shade they could find, panted, only lifting their heads long enough to glance in Lion Hunter's direction. The makeshift stick forms of empty meat-drying racks were everywhere, looking like giant grasshoppers.

Our hunters must have returned from a good-medicine buffalo kill.

There was too little breeze to keep away the clouds of flies, whose annoying numbers and unclean presence foretold an upcoming camp movement. Then, just as he came abreast of Willow's lodge, a large deerfly landed on the side of his nose and scurried toward his nostrils. Jerking sideways, Lion Hunter stumbled into one of the jerky racks, knocking it to the ground. It was his good fortune that the meat had already been removed from the rack, but a hoard of flies feasting on leftovers took instant flight—bad medicine. As he stumbled backward to avoid their swarm, his lance struck and knocked over a second rack. That launched yet another frenzied cloud of the darting insects and caused angry outcries from inside Willow's teepee.

Blood flooded his cheeks. His carefully laid-out plan ruined, Lion Hunter hurried away, his eyes solidly fixed on the ground before him. The sounds of many questions behind him cut through the heat of the day. Too embarrassed to respond, he fled to Kills-In-The-Dark's lodge at the far edge of the village.

Approaching hurriedly, he hailed his mentor.

"Hey ya, it is Lion Hunter," he called out softly, not wanting to attract any more attention to himself than he already had. A quick glance over his shoulder intensified his embarrassment as still more villagers converged upon the scene of his accident. Several dogs wove in among the growing crowd, excitedly looking for the source of the unusual fuss and maybe some scraps of meat.

He shifted back and forth on his feet, wishing for once, his mentor would respond quickly.

12

When Kills-In-The-Dark did not respond immediately to his request to enter her teepee, he stood rigid, looking straight ahead, trying to ignore the growing sounds of camp alarm behind him. Shamed that he had knocked over the meat-drying racks while self-importantly strutting by Willow's lodge, Lion Hunter was on the verge of fleeing the village when his mentor finally responded.

"Come." The sharpness of that single word was both timely and familiar. Lion Hunter let out a long breath and bent to enter.

He pushed aside the entrance flap while furtively glancing beneath his outstretched arm to see if the gathering crowd was moving in his direction. They were not, but several were looking his way, including Willow who stood separate from the others, fingering the single long braid of hair she always wore. He felt, more than saw, her dark eyes smiling at him.

His slung bow caught against the teepee's skin as he moved inside and he quickly removed it, setting it to the side.

"Sit," his mentor commanded when he finished lacing the bone pegs through the loops on the skin-covered entrance. "Tell me what things you have learned while journeying with Spirit Man."

Kills-In-The-Dark sat looking at him with open interest. Lion Hunter felt embarrassed—in the past she had always treated him with a formal kind of abruptness—she'd never before seemed this attentive.

"I have learned much," he responded, pausing a moment to consider his words before continuing. "Now I see the warrior in you with the light of Sun Boy, but not just that, I see the leader in you also." His words were warm with respect.

"Does the almost-warrior try to enchant the witch, now?" The look in her one good eye changed, just as attentive, but it had somehow become more severe. She did not mean for him to answer her question—Lion Hunter was sure of that. Over the months he had learned that she always spoke a bit more gruffly when pleased with his accomplishments. It was her way.

He decided not to smile at her crustiness, but the decision to hold back made him self-conscious, and he shifted uneasily to a new sitting position.

Tell me," she continued, "do the animals now speak to you as they do to Spirit Man?"

"Maybe they do not say so many things to me as they say to… him." Lion Hunter was still uncomfortable saying Spirit Man's name out loud—the old man was dead. "But I hear them and I see their moods now, where I did not before. I have learned many things, and Grandfather has promised I will learn many more. I am to meet with him tomorrow night so we can return to the wilderness for three more moons."

Head cocked to the side, Kills-In-The-Dark continued her study of him in silence. Lion Hunter found softness in the gesture but simply nodded his head and smiled, not knowing how else to respond to her continued interest and silent attention.

"So," she said after a long pause, "you have returned only to bring these compliments to me, or is there maybe another in our village you hope to see?"

Lion Hunter blushed.

How can she know about the girl that haunts my night visions? I have never told this to anyone, not even to Willow herself.

"I came to return the black gelding to your herd so … so Spirit Man and I can journey more quietly." He fidgeted. Saying, "the" black gelding, instead of "her" black gelding, was disrespectful.

"Have you named … the black gelding?" She watched him intently.

"Ahh … yes. I call him Black Storm," he answered, his voice ending in a near whisper.

It was bold of him to have named *her* horse… though he suspected she might gift the pony to him later.

"Good, this Black Storm is yours when you return from your vision quest."

Lion Hunter let his breath out, giddy with the anticipation of owning his own horse.

"Thank you, Aunt," he said softly.

She ignored his thanks. "I have spoken of your wolf dream to our holy man. Ghost Head says the eyes you saw are sent from the world beyond where all is spirit, and your dream is telling you they will watch over you during your vision quest. The wolf is a spirit, sent to you as a reminder that those who have great courage always protect their people, finding great respect among the spirit fathers when it is their turn to journey to the other side."

Lion Hunter leaned forward waiting, gaze fixed upon her lips—waiting.

"I have decided what place you will go to seek your Vision," Kills-In-The-Dark continued when Lion Hunter did not speak.

Her voice became formal again, that same familiar tone. His hopes that she would tell him where his quest would take him faded when she extended several slabs of jerked buffalo meat to him. The meat, wrapped loosely in a tattered elk-skin bag that was missing its cover flap, had been gifted to her in payment for medicinal help given to another.

Lion Hunter took the bag, setting it carefully to the ground beside him and waited.

"Do you wait for me to tell you where your vision quest will be? I will not. I will tell you when you have finished your journey to the west with Spirit Man. For now, your mind must be free of all foolish boy dreams. This is the learning way."

"West?" Her reference to a westward journey surprised him. "You know where Spirit Man and I go?" The old man had not told him their next destination.

"Yes. But now is not the time for talk of these things. You must go. Willow waits for you by a small spring a short walk in the wash behind my teepee."

Willow! How does she know these things? And why does Willow wait for me?

Lion Hunter sat, baffled, waiting for something—anything—more.

"Go," she barked, "do you wish her to wait forever?"

Lion Hunter knew questioning his mentor further would bring no more information. Bewildered, he rose, grabbed up his weapons and the jerky, and carefully unlaced the entrance skin while discreetly peeking out through its gaps. The bulk of the crowd had wandered away—leaving a small knot of close neighbors still standing near Willow's teepee and the fallen meat racks which, as of yet, had not been righted. Those who remained were laughing and joking among themselves.

"Hunter," Kills-In-The-Dark said softly. It had not been necessary for her to whisper—the others were not that near.

He turned to find out why she had done so. She was holding up the rear skirting of her teepee, pointing to the escape route with her chin.

Grateful, Lion Hunter released the entrance skin and crossed to the far side of her teepee. He carefully set his bow and the elk skin bag outside then, holding onto his lance, crawled beneath the skirt she held up, gathered his belongings, and climbed to his feet. A narrow path circled a huge spur of granite, then dropped away quickly in the direction of the arroyo. It took less time to find the wash than it would have taken to walk back by Willow's lodge. The person who used the path a short time earlier had collapsed the wash's steep sandy wall while descending to the dry creek bed below. In the bed, small scuffs left by that person's passage turned up-hill. Lion Hunter descended to the bottom of the wash with a series of sliding side steps, then paused as he looked in both directions and examined the floor of the wash more closely.

Bushes like water, water likes low points.

He looked up the wash for its source—a short distance away a promising line of vegetation poured out of a large crack in the vertical granite wall. The floor of the earth there looked like it might be flat enough for a pool to form at its bottom. Lion Hunter kneeled and scooped a shallow trench into the sand. It was damp. He stood and moved in the direction of the crack.

He found her sitting just below the fractured granite wall, her back to a small pool of seep water. She sat knees together, and hands neatly folded into the softness of her doeskin dress. Thick black hair surrounded her round face, a breeze stirring unattended strands, the tips of which swirled up in front of her face. He stopped, mute … unable to conjure words to fit the first-ever moment of privacy between them and the first time he had seen her with her hair down. A bolt of edgy excitement shot through Lion Hunter's chest.

They had never had a real conversation outside the presence of her parents or giggling friends. Their relationship was little more than a series of haunting gazes—hers—and nervously averted eyes—his. Now it was she who lowered her eyes.

"I have only seen your hair in a braid before," he said, words tumbling out of his mouth without thought.

"Do you like it like this?" she asked, smiling as she brushed several strands of hair away from her eyes.

Lion Hunter's breath drained from his chest. He sucked in more air, and held it, trying to find the words he needed to answer her question.

Her voice is a breeze among cottonwoods, the softest trickle of a brook. In all of my world it is the most beautiful sound ever.

"I thought we must speak together, alone," she said, now looking directly into his eyes.

Make a good posture for her. You stand like a fool.

He nodded but still found no words.

"Hunter, we have little time. You must talk to me."

"I go to my vision quest soon," he blurted. "I will be a warrior and…"

"And you will have your own lodge and take a wife, yes?"

He puffed up his chest. "Yes." The single word burst from him so forcefully he became embarrassed for himself. He looked away, focusing on a water bug making tiny rippling circles on the pond's surface.

"Hunter," she bent forward, looking up at him, "will I be your wife?"

He raised his head, stunned, seeking any sign that she made fun of him. But he lost all-purpose when his gaze came to rest on the dark beauty of her wide-set, subtly slanted, eyes.

Willow, you have the most beautiful eyes in….

"Yes," he erupted with so much joy he completely forgot about his almost-warrior pride.

"I want that also, Hunter. Come back for me." Smiling, she stood and took his hands in hers. Then, looking up into his eyes again, she said, "Will you do that for me?"

"I will return and you will be my wife," he responded, his insides flushing with sincerity.

Willow gazed at him for a long moment, and then smiled so softly his breath caught with joy. Eyes still locked to his, she pulled the hand up and pressed it down over her heart. He felt its pounding rhythm, the rise and fall of her chest as she breathed. When she lifted her other hand to his chest he closed his own over it and let his eyes close as he drank in the happiness her touch brought into his life. Both stood motionless, unwilling to violate the moment with the clumsiness of movement.

"Two hearts together," Willow whispered.

"Two hearts together," Lion Hunter whispered back.

When next she moved it was to pull her hands away while whispering urgently, "Hunter, we must part for now. Others must not see us alone together."

The abrupt separation brought disappointment but gave rise to a question that had been pressing against his thoughts.

"Willow, tell me, how do you come to be here and how did Kills-In-The-Dark know about us or that you would be here?"

"When I did not see you in camp for many days, my heart grew lonely, so I went to the medicine woman to ask after you. She told me you went to the wilderness with Spirit Man for a teaching journey."

Lion Hunter was stunned.

"How can you speak of the dead like this?"

"Silly, he is not dead. My father says it is foolish to pretend the old one is dead when everyone knows he is alive. And my mother agrees."

Lion Hunter knew she was right, but many in their village did not believe as they did, and speaking so casually about the old man still made him feel uncomfortable. He shifted his feet, glancing back down the arroyo.

"Anyway," Willow continued, her nose wrinkling playfully, "your mentor told me to come to this spot when I heard you return…"

Lion Hunter looked down at the ground.

"I ran to this place to wait for you," she added quickly.

The reference to hearing him tripping over the drying racks caused a flush of shame, but she reached up and touched his cheek. "Should a proud warrior become so embarrassed before his adoring almost-wife?" she asked, smiling up at him.

Lion Hunter took a deep breath, shook his head, and willed his embarrassment away.

"I will be a fine husband and you will be my Willow," he asserted with the loving manner in which Spirit Man spoke of his daughter, flashing in his mind.

She again took both of his hands in hers.

"Yes, and we must both quickly go now, before we are discovered. I will wait with much excitement for your next return, my brave Lion Hunter."

"I will make a fine wife to you, I promise," she called back over her shoulder as she hurried down the wash.

"Good bye," he responded to her back, heart pounding.

I will bring you the finest furs, my sweet Willow. I will bring meats, and I will protect you and …

13

On his way out of camp, Lion Hunter circled around its edges to avoid being seen. He was excited and wanted the time alone to daydream about being a warrior and having Willow as his wife. The thrill and anticipation of this new twist in his life was bursting inside him. He felt like running madly across the grass-covered hills, shouting and jumping with a joy he had not felt since childhood. On the outside however, he struggled to remain calm—to maintain a look of warrior-like dignity.

The effort, though, was too great. Nerves tingling, he stopped, looked all around and, deciding no one else was within sight or hearing, he began to dance wildly. He kept time to his dancing by imagining the drumbeats and chants real warriors cavorted to when dancing around late-night campfires as they celebrated the exploits of past raids.

These steps were his own, made-up and memorized in many private moments of practice. He'd rehearsed and saved them so he could have his own dance after becoming a warrior, but he was so excited now, he couldn't hold them in any longer.

He stopped abruptly. Still excited, he spun his head, not really sure what he was looking for. When he spotted the distant wall of the cutoff meadow, where he'd turned Black Storm loose earlier in the day, he knew what he had to do. Lion Hunter broke into a mad run across the open plain, slowing only when he drew near the dry river channel's bank.

There, he dropped to the ground and clambered up to the wall's edge, raking his eyes over the village herd below. Black Storm and the rest of Kills-In-The-Dark's tiny herd were not far from where he'd left them earlier, and all the near pasture boys were gathered in a group playing the sticks game. He scrambled to the valley concealed within the shadows of the rock wall. Lion Hunter, almost-warrior, smiled, smug in using the stealthy skills Grandfather taught him as he slinked through the larger herd, moving toward Black Storm and the others.

The lead mare, head lifted and nostrils flared, had been checking his progress since he appeared on the rim of the river wall. The rest of her group, seeing no alert in her, kept grazing.

"Black Storm, it is Lion Hunter, your new master," Lion Hunter whispered as he reached the gelding's side. "After I complete my vision quest and made a good raid, I will be a warrior. Then I will have my own lodge and Willow will be my wife, and you will be my favorite war pony. You will be at the entrance to my teepee, and we will always be ready to defend our people." The pony's ears pricked and swiveled as his dark head moved around nervously.

Lion Hunter smiled. "Ahh, yes, you sense my joy and look for its cause. But you do not know Willow or that she has made me this excited. You have fine senses my friend, and we will be safe together for many years."

I know father, I know. A warrior must always remain calm around his pony so it does not become confused about what is important to pay attention to.

"I will let you graze. I must go with Spirit Man to learn more so that I will be a fine fox walker and the best warrior of our people."

Still churned inside, he pressed his forehead to the pony's nose, said goodbye and slipped back out of the grassy cut-off valley— still unseen by the pasture boys.

He took a visual bearing on the distant hill where he was to meet Spirit Man and began trotting toward the sun, which was already beginning its drop to the ridgeline of the mountains. Lion Hunter's thoughts filled with new purpose.

I should have guessed we would travel west when he selected that hill. I forgot to use my think-habit. But I am returning a day early now, so let him be surprised when we meet tomorrow morning.

Still far enough away to remain undetected, Lion Hunter turned south and continued his jogging, then west and finally, after he passed the meeting hill, north again. As darkness neared, he began making his final approach to the hill. He crawled slowly, careful to remain concealed by shrubbery so Spirit Man would not see his arrival. He smiled to himself, knowing Spirit Man would expect him to arrive from the other side of the hill.

You do not expect me until tomorrow, old man. Now, I will surprise you for a change.

He halted when he found the right spot. Soon the sun would disappear behind the towering wall of the Rockies and daylight would begin to fade. That was good—he would stay here until early the next morning.

Lion Hunter knew when Spirit Man would be settling himself into his own secluded position to watch for Lion Hunter's approach. He was even reasonably sure where that position would be. The young almost-warrior calculated Spirit Man's hiding spot would be near the thick rock spine descending the hill's east side—the place Spirit Man pointed to when telling Lion Hunter where he would wait.

In the morning I will get there first and make a nice surprise place to wait for you, old man.

Smiling to himself, Lion Hunter crawled into a tiny clearing walled in by thick brush—well down from the hill's crest and rock outcropping. He lay down and, removing the sheepskin-decorated shirt his mother had made from his pack, snuggled it beneath his head as a pillow against the earth's hardness.

In the morning the old fox will see the fine skills of the young fox.

"There is a more comfortable sleeping spot a small distance from here."

Startled to an upright sitting position, Lion Hunter turned and, found Spirit Man within arm's length.

The old man was lying on his back with his hands clasped behind his head. There was pleasantness in his demeanor as he smiled up at his young apprentice.

Lips clenched shut, Lion Hunter pitched himself back to the ground and rolled back to his original position, facing away from his teacher. He could not bear the embarrassment of speaking to Spirit Man at the moment. Almost immediately Spirit Man's quiet snoring started. Fuming, Lion Hunter got little sleep that night.

* * *

The young brave had not yet opened his eyes when Spirit Man commented on the exuberance of a fox sparrow singing nearby.

"This one sings of his joy, of finding food enough to feed himself and his family. Do you hear that other, farther down there?" He pointed to a scrawny patch of serviceberry bushes lower on the slope. "There are many more fox sparrows, there and there. He pointed to several different locations around them. "Each knows he must not come near to the place of another or eat that other's food. This hillside is their village, and they all hear each other and they listen to learn when hunters come among them.

"Yesterday, when you were sneaking up this hill, this little bird," he said pointing to the nearby singer, "quit his song and made soft 'chip' alarms and all these that I have pointed to became silent, waiting to find out what hunter had come among them to take away their joy. At first I did not know where the one who alarmed was because I could not see him, but I could see another over by the rocks." Again he pointed, this time with his chin.

"So I saw that other, and he was looking at this singer, this one that yesterday was chipping. All the birds wished to find out how their neighbor would act so they watched him to know what danger was here.

"When I saw this one he was staring down the hill. And so I knew where the hunter was, and I came and found you preparing for your sleep in this not-so-soft sleeping place.

"It is a fine morning. We go now," he finished.

With that, the old exile grabbed up his pack and silently picked his way through the surrounding brush. Outside the thicket, Spirit Man began walking toward the distant western mountains. Lion Hunter grabbed up his pack and weapons and scrambled to catch up.

"You must always listen to the sounds of the animal people so you can know where the hunters are," Spirit Man said when Lion Hunter caught up to him.

"But yesterday I was not hunting you when I lay down to sleep," Lion Hunter quibbled.

"So tell me what was in your heart as you came to that place?" Spirit Man smiled, knowing the answer already.

"I thought to sneak up on you, Grandfather."

"And does the coyote not look like a hunter when he sneaks? Sneaking is the way of the hungry among all of Mother Earth's people."

Lion Hunter fell into step beside the old man, remembering a long-ago conversation with Kills-In-The-Dark about a deer and the difference between a hunter who lies on the ground and another who tries to sneak up on his prey.

It is the way the hunter moves, how he sneaks, that tells the deer he hunts, that he is hungry.

Late that day the two came to a small stream. They stopped to drink and rest in the cooling shade provided by a stand of cottonwood trees. Lion Hunter looked around at the surrounding territory, which was new to him. He removed his moccasins and put his feet into the water, then laid his head back on his pack.

"This is called Sheep Eater stream, named after the Sheep Eater people who are called the Snake Nation by others. I think because of the wiggling sign we make to name our people in sign talk," Spirit Man said, interrupting Lion Hunter's quiet. "The Sheep Eaters are our people—those we meet with each year in the time of our tribe's Great Gathering.

"I came here with your father three winters ago," the old man continued, squatting beside Lion Hunter. "We met a group of Sheep Eaters here and traded a wolverine winter-bonnet to them for the beautiful winter-pelt of a mountain sheep. Your father wanted the pelt to gift to your mother. But she did not keep his present. Instead she used it to make one of her fine Crow shirts and gave it back to him. It is that shirt you carry in your pack and use for a pillow."

Lion Hunter reached back and pressed his hand against his pack to feel the shirt's bulge. Softness came over him and he closed his eyes, wondering where his mother might be, if she was still alive and safe.

Spirit Man and Lion Hunter traveled west for four days then north for three more before ascending into thickly forested woodlands with strange earth holes that held boiling water and spouted great clouds of steam. They passed large herds of elk, many small groups of buffalo—mostly bulls—and streams and rivers too many to count. Every valley had beaver dams, and they saw both black and grizzly bears, which they circled to avoid confrontation.

There were wolves, and he saw several big horn sheep high up on the craggy mountainsides that surrounded the lush lowlands.

There was more game than Lion Hunter had ever seen in one place before. It excited him to think about the fine hunts he could have here.

"Why do our people live out on the plains and not here, Grandfather?"

"It is a hard place to live, Lion Hunter. Mother Earth has made this land beautiful and rich with all things people want, so many tribes come here and want to stay. But that makes much war because people do not share well.

"After our band began trading ponies from the pierced-nose people of the plateaus nations, we moved away from our brothers, the Sheep Eaters. We became buffalo hunters on the plains. At first there was less warfare with other tribes. But soon others traded for ponies and they came to the plains also—and our people and their people argued over hunting grounds. That is how the Crow came to be our enemy, and the Blackfeet and others too.

"When we became plainsmen we began calling ourselves the Wolf Ridge people because White Mountain was the sacred center of our band's new great circle and Wolf Ridge was the most beautiful place on that mountain.

"We will explore this place for a time then return to the Wolf Ridge people so you can go on your vision quest."

14

The ridgeline was spotted with dignified whitebark pine that looked down over a wide valley of rolling lowlands and faded off so far into the distance that, buffalo grazing there looked no larger than ants. Spirit Man, with Lion Hunter following, turned off the ridge taking a narrow elk trail that meandered down through a thick forest of lodgepole pine and aspen stands still bright with summer's crisp green leaves. The path wound through the timber, crossing and re-crossing a small stream that wandered down from a seep-spring where Spirit Man and Lion Hunter stopped to drink, farther up the mountainside.

Just above the valley floor, the two were surprised to find another whitebark pine. This one, twisted and stunted from its struggle for life so far down the mountain from the rest of its stately kindred, was still healthy enough to provide shade for the two to rest under. Both sat down beneath its fragrant canopy, their legs dangling over the crumbling granite ledge from which it grew.

"Did you hear that noisy bird as we came to his tree here?" Spirit Man asked, canting his head toward a gnarled branch of the pine that hung far out over the valley floor below.

"I heard. It was a tree creeper, Grandfather."

Lion Hunter had been listening to the bird sing its song as they approached the shade pine. He watched when it fled up the slope to a nearby aspen and perched peering back at them in silence.

The old man responded with a satisfied grunt, wiggled into a more comfortable position, and looked out over the scene below them. Lion Hunter also scanned the valley, wondering what things Spirit Man might see that he would not.

The drop to the valley from here is four times my height. It is dangerous to sit here, but if Spirit Man sits here so do I.

Eastward, the valley stretched out of sight becoming broader and more thinly vegetated until, far in the distance, sage dominated. That is where the buffalo were, tiny black dots among the scattered sage. The west end of the valley floor was lush, a carpet of grass surrounding a beaver dam reinforced by the huge carcass of a lodgepole pine that had fallen there long ago. A gentle stream, flowing out of the forest edge a short distance beyond, fed the pond.

The smaller stream they crisscrossed during their descent tumbled off the mountainside and joined water escaping the beaver pond below. From there the water continued down the valley as a broad rocky shallow.

The tree creeper returned to a limb on the other side of their shade pine and, ignoring the two humans, once again began singing its song.

In silence, Spirit Man stuck two fingers out, pointing them toward Lion Hunter's eyes. The gesture was abbreviated, measured in its delivery. When Lion Hunter looked up the old man pointed those same fingers toward the valley floor.

Grandfather signs slowly so he does not attract the eyes of others with his movement.

"Fox, play," the old man signed gracefully, his lips pursed to signal silence.

Lion Hunter immediately picked out movement in the grass on the near side of the pond. A litter of fox kits were play-attacking one another, a frenzy of pouncing, nipping fur balls. One leaped down upon his littermates from a nearby boulder and immediately scrambled back up the rock and leapt again.

Below their rocky overhang, midway across the valley floor, a mustang stallion grazed on a small rise, his white speckled rump facing away from them. Periodically the animal raised its head and glanced at them, then, still chewing, gazed in the direction of the foxes. Farther east, in the dell behind the stallion's knoll, four mares stood drinking from a shallow pool afforded by the stream.

"Watch, fox ears," the old man signed. Lion Hunter studied the foxes, at first not seeing anything unusual but after a moment he noticed the ears of each periodically twitch toward the beaver pond while they cavorted, though none had yet allowed whatever they were hearing to interfere with their frolicking. Eventually, one, his teeth locked tight to the nape of another's neck, rolled his eyes in the same direction all their ears had been turning and immediately let his litter mate go. When he stopped to stare the others did as well.

"The tree creeper has stopped his song," Spirit Man whispered. "He tells us what the foxes tell us."

The stallion immediately lifted his head. His ears swiveled forward as he turned his body to face the direction in which the fox kits were staring. The stallion's attention was focused on the edge of the forest beyond the foxes. The mares had not yet alerted, but when one lifted her muzzle from the water and looked up at the stallion, all four immediately began climbing the incline, moving closer to the stallion.

Lion Hunter examined the area beyond the pond where all were looking. He mentally noted that the tree creeper remained silent. He concentrated on the thick tangle of serviceberry brush at the edge of the forest.

As Lion Hunter watched, a second-year black bear forced his forequarters out of the thick brush and stopped, his tan muzzle stained with the dark purple of the bush's berries.

Three deer fled nearby shadows, and the entire litter of fox kits tried to mount the boulder at once, wanting a better view of the threat they detected. The vixen, previously not visible, stood up on her hind legs—upper body poking up out of the thick grass near her kits. She spotted the bear, and the entire family immediately melted into the forest.

The stallion lifted his head sampling the breeze, snorted, looked one last time in the bear's direction then turned and trotted down the rise. The mares had begun moving away when he snorted and were already well ahead of him.

"Tell me, young almost-warrior, what did you see?"

Lion Hunter pondered the events he witnessed for a suitable period before speaking.

"I saw the animals tell each other a bear was near."

"Why a bear?"

"When he came from the forest he was downwind. The other animals did not see or smell him, but the deer and foxes probably heard his loud foraging sounds. Other predators would be more silent, I think."

"True. And the mares?"

"They did not see the bear, but they knew danger was near. The mares saw the stallion's look-alarm and knew he saw other animals that were alerting, then, when he snorted, they knew that he saw the danger himself. But Grandfather, I do not understand why the beaver family did not slap their tails and swish the water."

"We will look, but I think maybe the beaver family is not there anymore. Do you see the water current on this side of the dam? Their dam is broken."

* * *

Spirit Man called the territory they traveled through the land-of-boiling-mud, and they remained to explore its strange and beautiful landscape for many days. In that time, they saw a great black cliff with broken rock chunks littering its base. The fractured surfaces of these rocks were so smooth they gleamed like sunlight shining on dark water.

This is the rock Pony Man calls Night Stone. He uses it to make his finest points for trade to our hunters in exchange for meat, when they return from hunts.

Spirit Man sifted through the debris and selected several chunks to tuck away in the pouches of his carry sack.

So, the old storyteller gets his Night Stone from my teacher. And what gift does Spirit Man get in return, I wonder?

In a broad flat river valley, another feature of the strange land they were exploring, Spirit Man taught Lion Hunter how to build barriers of rock that funneled fish into shallow waters they could not escape. They speared many with sharpened tree branches and caught others with their hands. Lion Hunter was astonished when the old man took him to a nearby boiling-water hole and taught him to dip the fish into it on the tips of their makeshift spears. They cooked their catch and had a delicious supper.

The teachings of this journey greatly changed the way Lion Hunter saw his world. He no longer just saw a rabbit sitting quietly beneath a bush or a meadowlark silently looking in a single direction. Instead, he saw complete stories for each—tales that explained all that surrounded the creature and its activities in that moment. The napping coyote was no longer just tired. He was a cunning hunter whose alert ears and twitching nose always remained awake. He was a predator who napped, yes, but one who napped near a prudently selected trail, a trail sniffed thoroughly to locate the freshest and greatest concentration of his prey's scent—prey that would soon be his next meal.

At his teacher's direction, Lion Hunter lurked days on end in the ambush spots of the wilderness's most stealthy predators. He curled up this time in a bobcat lay, or on another occasion, beneath the low-hanging branches of a whitebark pine in a she-lion's territory.

He and Spirit Man discovered the lion's ambush spot by backtracking her sign from a debris-covered deer carcass they found. They first tracked her back to the kill site from which she dragged the deer to the cache. From there they tracked her back to her original ambush lay. Together Lion Hunter and Spirit Man studied each of the sites and their surroundings until both were satisfied they fully understood why she selected that site to await her prey's arrival.

"She smells the deer scent on the trail first," Spirit Man said, "like our camp dogs. But deer scent is in every part of the forest. To make her excited to hunt, deer scent must be very fresh and also heavy with many recent comings and goings of deer. She is like a dog that smells everything but becomes excited only when scent tells its nose, not just that food was here, but that food recently came and went by here many times."

Lion Hunter learned to listen to the undercurrents of wilderness creatures' voices so he would recognize their joys, their fears, and their many other moods.

"Be the mouse," Spirit Man told him, "if you want to understand the mouse's ways."

And in the ways Spirit Man taught him, Lion Hunter came to understand not just when menace prowled nearby or when the moment was harmless but also how differently each animal reacted to their presence.

But, thrilling as learning the secret ways of the wilderness was, the opportunity to endlessly probe Sprit Man for more stories of Kills-In-The-Dark's prowess were even more so. Spirit Man told many stories of her years in the wilderness and with Lion Hunter's people since.

"Once," he said, "when my Pigeon was digging wild onions in the field with another wife of our band, two Crow warriors came upon them. The warriors were returning from hunting and had a fat deer draped over a third pony's back.

"These warriors wanted to taunt our Wolf Ridge women. They made fun of my Pigeon's scarred face and both caused their ponies to make nervous steps close to her feet. They kicked at her with their own feet to try to make her run away, but she would not leave her friend. When they found no more fun in this, both went to the other woman. One of these Crows leaped to the ground from his pony and threw her to the ground while the other sat on his pony watching and laughing.

"When the attacker began ripping away the woman's clothing, my brave daughter threw herself on his back and cut his throat with a single slice from her knife. Before his friend could grab her, my Pigeon leaped on the dead warrior's pony and raced away. The second Crow chased her.

"My daughter returned after a short while, leading the other warrior's pony, so when the two women rode into to the Wolf Ridge camp that afternoon, they brought with them three fine Crow ponies and fresh venison. When Pony Man heard about this killing, he went to Kills-In-The-Dark to learn the story so he could tell it to all around the storyteller-fire."

"But Grandfather, how did she get the other Crow warrior's pony?"

"I do not know, but I think maybe he did not trade it to her for wild onions," the old man said, chuckling.

The tales of her deeds were gripping and, in the end, Lion Hunter came to think of his medicine-woman mentor not simply as cunning and skilled in the use of weapons but as one of the bravest warriors of their band. She would never allow fear in her heart to interfere with what needed to be done.

* * *

Lion Hunter and Spirit Man sat across from one another at a small fire, both staring down into its red embers. A duck, caught earlier that evening, sizzled on a flat rock placed among the fire's coals.

"It is three moons since our journey began," Spirit Man said, still staring down into the fire.

Lion Hunter waited patiently for any more the old man might want to say.

"I think it is time. How do you think?" The old man speared each of the pieces of meat with a sharpened twig and turned them over then glanced up at Lion Hunter. He licked the juice from one stick's end and smiled.

"This duck is fat and greasy, he eats well and was ready for the chill of Cold Maker's return, I think," he added before Lion Hunter responded to his question.

The young man nodded, acknowledging the question, and then looked back down into the fire—lips pursed and head nodding slowly as he pondered his response. It was time, he had no doubt of that, but impulsiveness was behind him now—he was ready to be a man. Thoughtful answers were men's gifts to others. They were the custom of the elders among his people, and they would be his custom from this time on.

"It is time, Grandfather," he answered after a suitable pause.

During the next week, as they made their way back to the village, Spirit Man fell back into the role of companion, just as he had with so many of the camp's adults, one at a time in the wilderness, over the years.

Both enjoyed the journey. Spirit Man following, allowing Lion Hunter to make all travel decisions on his own—when to hunt, where to camp, and how long to walk each day. Lion Hunter's confidence matured, even in these few last days. He felt less the student and more the man with each decision.

They found the village's current camp without effort and, as always, Spirit Man paused at a distance from the camp to return to his penance for the misdeed he had committed so long ago.

"Lion Hunter," he said before they parted, "not every brave goes on a vision quest. The man who killed your father did not. All his people knew he could never be trusted to provide for a family or to protect his people in time of great need—the two forever-honors of all warriors. So no one trained him, and he did not know the honor of seeking and finding the meaning of his own life." In the silence that followed Spirit Man's powerful statement, Lion Hunter waited, his entire being focused on what might come next.

"The Grandfathers of the spirit world honor you with this time in your life. You must make your people proud. Go, seek your vision, and return to your people with the heart of a warrior."

Not daring to speak, Lion Hunter nodded and tightened the muscles of his face against the urge to tear up. He did not understand the emotion fully, but he felt it, and he knew Spirit Man would forever be a powerful knot in the stitching that bound his life together.

15

"Hey, ya, Aunt," Lion Hunter hailed from outside Kills-In-The-Dark's teepee. "It is Hunter. I am back from my teaching in the wilderness, and I would speak with you." After leaving Spirit Man, he'd come directly to his mentor's lodge, too anxious to start on his vision quest even to search for Willow.

"It is a deep voice I hear—can this be my almost-warrior?" she replied. "Come, come quick. Let me see you."

Brimming with pride, Lion Hunter sucked in a full chest of air, bent and entered her lodge. The teepee's heavy aroma of herbs, roasted seeds and pitch immediately flooded his senses, rekindling feelings of security and gladness from their past together. In his father's teepee, the smell of wood ash was always more prevalent – because of his mother's work on leathers, he knew.

I guess Kills-In-The-Dark is my family now. The thought brought revelation—the loss of his father and mother no longer poked so sharply at his heart.

He pulled himself upright, respectfully waiting for his mentor to invite him to sit.

"So," she said, squinting up at him, "I think you are maybe taller now. Sit down so my neck does not break looking up."

The young man sat, grinning, unable to conceal his pride while this woman who was his new family carefully folded away a soft rabbit skin containing the dogbane seeds she had been grinding.

"You grind dogbane seeds. Is there a new baby in our village?"

She took up her mortar and pestle, smiling to herself as she carefully tucked the items away in a leather pack dangling by its strap from the shadows above. She was proud of his learning.

"Young Fish has weakness, she said, holding a smile back, "in his head, I think."

Lion Hunter smiled at her joke.

"So, do all the animal nations now tremble in hiding places that are no longer hiding places because the great almost-warrior finds them?"

His smile widened.

The two laughed and joked together, comfortable in being reunited. Lion Hunter enjoyed himself and was very pleased that she now allowed him to speak so casually with her, but always his thoughts returned to his vision quest. He did not raise the subject as she was his mentor, and she alone would decide when to speak of that.

After what seemed to him a long while, she stopped speaking and looked across at him, her expression serious.

"I have spoken to the holy man about your wolf-dream." It always seemed odd to Lion Hunter when she spoke of her husband at a distance, but, at this moment, he was less interested in their relationship than he was in the importance of Ghost Head's interpretation of his wolf-dream. Lion Hunter held his breath while his mentor stared down into the black ashes of her fire circle.

"After two days he returned to me and told me your dream's meaning. He said the Spirit Fathers have sent this dream-wolf to call you to Wolf Ridge on our people's most sacred mountain. That is where your vision and the meaning of your life waits for you."

Lion Hunter sat silent, heart racing, hoping to be told he could leave on his vision quest immediately.

Kills-In-The-Dark reached inside the hanging pack at her side, and pulled the mortar and pestle back out. Still holding both in her hand, she lifted her eyes to his.

"There is a young girl, I think, who would speak with you before you leave."

Lion Hunter nodded, so excited he could hardly contain himself. Still waiting politely, he remained sitting.

Still, she does not tell me I can leave.

"Go, then," she said after a pause, waving her hand dismissively toward the teepee's entrance.

He leaped to his feet, spun, and threw back the entrance flap but nearly fell trying to stop when he heard her clear her throat.

Still looking up, she spoke softly to him.

"I am proud for you, Hunter. You will be a fine warrior—my pretty warrior."

He had never been so proud in his life. Striding toward his lean-to, he felt as though the eyes of every villager must be watching him.

He stopped at his lean-to only long enough to empty his pack of the last of the rabbit he and Spirit Man dried for their return trip. He hung the unneeded meat over the structure's frame. As Spirit Man had instructed, he would be fasting for the next several days. He also left the crude spear made to fish with during his time in the land of boiling mud. A knife would be his only weapon on the vision quest.

He gave the rabbit to Kills-In-The-Dark then trotted off toward the center of camp, carrying his travel pack.

Willow's family was poor by village standards. Her father, Stone Shirt, had been severely gored by a buffalo in a hunting accident years earlier. He owned only one horse, gifted to him by his friend, Chief Weasel Bear. There were no other males in his lodge to help provide for his family. His teepee was smaller than most, made of mismatched skins gifted over time by more successful lodges.

Lion Hunter did not know exactly where her lodge would be, so, once he came to the center of camp, he looked for and found Camp Chief Weasel Bear's lodge. Glancing around, he found her lodge, then stopped before it and hailed her father.

"Uncle Stone Shirt, it is Lion Hunter, I would speak to your daughter, Willow."

From inside, he heard Willow's mother's grunt her disdain. The wait, before she pulled back the entrance flap and stared out at him, was disrespectful. From behind the mother, Willow peeked out, her face heavily shadowed by the interior gloom of the teepee.

"My daughter is not here. Why do you ask to speak to her?"

Behind her mother's back Willow signed, "Arroyo. Go."

His conversation with the woman who he hoped would be is mother-in-law was brief. Both mother and father, he knew, hoped to marry their daughter off to a successful warrior, one who could help support the family. They were not interested in the son of a Crow slave-wife, now orphaned and living with the village witch.

Lion Hunter excused himself and rushed to the wash where the two had met in what seemed to him a lifetime ago. The village camp had been moved since then, but only a short distance.

Upon reaching the seep water pool, he sat on the same rock she had three months earlier and waited nervously. He let his fingers glide over the rock, touching the surface where her hand had been, imagining their fingers intertwined.

The waiting seemed forever, but when she flew around the last turn of the wash and rushed up to him, his world was new like a first rain.

He leaped to his feet and she threw her arms around his shoulders, pressing her head to his chest. Lion Hunter stood motionless, full of joy but too self-conscious to wrap his own arms around her.

"I am so glad that you came to see me before you left," she gushed, now leaning back and looking up into his eyes. Lion Hunter looked back, his own awkward smile somehow surviving the heart pounding excitement of their second-ever touch. He remembered the first, when they placed their hands over each other's hearts.

"Do you still wish to take me as your wife?" she asked, wide eyes looking up into his.

Lion Hunter's head bobbed, but he could not find the words to speak.

"Kills-In-The Dark told me you will make a fine warrior and a good husband. Actually, she said you will be a pretty warrior."

Lion Hunter blushed.

"I will be a proud wife to you." Willow hesitated, "My father speaks to Beaver about taking me as a second wife because our lodge is poor. So you must become a warrior soon and save me." She looked up through the loose strands of her hair, eyes appealing.

"I will come back and we will be married," Lion Hunter said, new purpose filling his breast.

They parted quickly and Lion Hunter, newly resolved to the urgency of becoming both man and warrior, immediately left camp.

* * *

As he walked, he went back over a story Grandfather told him while the two of them camped at Sheep Eater creek. It was about the movement of his people to the plains. During the story Grandfather cut nine sticks, notching them successively, each representing a single day's travel. He carved them just as his people had always done when journeying to new lands. The travelers gathered around others of their tribe who made journeys into the new country.

The first stick, the one with a single notch, he lay down in soft dirt facing the same direction his people walked in when they left Sheep Eater creek. Spirit Man drew each river that intersected that stick into the dirt at its proper distance from the creek. Likewise, he drew in the hills and valleys, the different types of vegetation, and all locations where water could be found. Every unique and significant feature of the surrounding environment was detailed in the dirt for Lion Hunter to understand how the sticks could guide him. When the fifth stick was laid out, Grandfather poked a finger into the dirt next to it and looked up with a questioning expression.

"That is the hill we left to start our journey here," Lion Hunter said immediately, letting Spirit Man know he was following the lesson. Lion Hunter memorized his people's route to the holy mountain and all of the landmarks along the way—just as inexperienced young raiders did when instructed by experienced warriors for raids to distant lands where they had never before traveled. When he was done memorizing the features, he carved each into the proper day's stick, he bundled them and placed them in his pack.

Lion Hunter used his memory of those land features, and the sticks, for his and Spirit Man's return trip. He easily relocated the abandoned Wolf Ridge camp they'd left from three months earlier. From there, it was easy to track the sign left behind by the whole village, to this new Wolf Ridge camp.

From the moment Kills-In-The-Dark told him he was to go to Wolf Ridge and White Mountain for his vision quest, Lion Hunter understood why Grandfather told him that story. He also knew the mountain was four days' travel from the present Wolf Ridge camp.

He had never before traveled to the sacred mountain, but he had directions, and like all plains people he intuitively understood the plains landscape—he would find it easily.

Lion Hunter walked quickly away from the village, eager to reach his destination and begin his vision quest. He carried only a daypack, a knife, and fire-making tools for emergencies. He had no need of food—he would fast until completing his manhood-trial. He would find water at those places Spirit Man had shown him on his journey map, at least until he arrived at the holy mountain. From that point he would quit taking water also—Grandfather told him this was necessary to cleanse his mind of real world thoughts so the Spirit Fathers might recognize his worthiness and quickly send him his vision and life purpose.

While walking, he remembered a vision he had had two years before at fourteen. It happened when he was being hunted by Cut Nose, the she-lion the War Chief Carries-His-Lion had pulled from his pony and fought with.

Coyote man, the trickster, came to him in the dark that time. He hadn't really seen Coyote man then, only heard him, but to Lion Hunter it was a vision anyway, one he'd kept secret ever since.

Now, as he walked, he was excited and wanted to share this, the most important journey of his life, so badly he decided to speak to Coyote Man.

"Hey, ya, Coyote Man, I think maybe you do not dare to mock me now. I am soon to be a warrior. Look." He pointed out over the rolling brush covered rises and depressions before him. "Do you see that doe antelope there? She has a fawn hiding in the sage somewhere nearby. If we watched her like the real coyote does, eventually she would lead us to her fawn which she must return to nurse twice during each day." He rambled on with no other purpose than to brag about his newly developed understanding of nature.

"I am fasting so that I might be more ready for the vision my totem animal-person is sent to gift to me."

The thrill of speaking to a vision who would not speak back, however, wore off quickly and the ever present need to be alert while moving across the open plain soon settled him back into silence. Even so, his mind was awash with future warrior thoughts.

That evening, when he stopped, he built a fire and pretended to eat. Then, after the full darkness of night arrived, he silently picked up his possessions and sneaked to a different location so that anyone who might be watching him set up camp would not know where he was.

During the second day he became hungry. He saw many rabbits and a whole prairie dog town with a badger and coyote so busy working together to catch one of the colony's inhabitants neither paid any attention to him. The badger dug furiously while the cunning coyote, having snuck up close to his hunting partner, sniffed the dirt flung from its growing trench. After identifying the scent of that particular prairie dog, it was easy for the coyote to distinguish its exit holes from those of the rest of the prairie dogs.

I think the coyote will have dinner tonight. Maybe not the badger.

Continuing on his journey, Lion Hunter traveled steadily during the rest of the day, carefully matching his memory of the journey map to the surrounding land features. He found himself comfortably remembering exactly how far he had to travel to keep on pace—one day, one stick. By afternoon he found the line of cottonwood trees Grandfather drew for that day's map and studied them carefully. He decided the greenest of them, near the far end of the valley, would be where he had the best chance of finding water. While still at a safe distance, he crawled to the top of a rise and watched a long while for any movement. Once certain no others watched, he walked in among the trees and set up his camp. After a brief rest, he went to find water.

He found it in the sandy bottom of the dry river channel after digging down to the depth of his elbow. The seep water was cool and delicious. He'd passed up the only other watering spot on this day's journey because a deer carcass fouled it.

During his third day of travel, hunger repeatedly pushed its way into his consciousness. He conjured the taste of duck, remembering the one he and Spirit Man roasted over an open fire at Sheep Eater creek. His mouth watered when, in his memory, it dripped its succulent fats down onto the crackling embers beneath. Cooing doves brought unconscious saliva and began a series of imagined meals that drew his attention away from the needs of safe plains travel. By the end of that day, his stomach was ballooned with water he'd drank to chase away its emptiness. He was still hungry.

The fourth day was much the same.

He was surprised midmorning on the fifth day when it finally occurred to him that he was no longer hungry. He was standing at the foot of the sacred mountain making his way along an elk trail that hugged a sheer rock wall on one side and dropped sharply down into a river valley on the other.

16

Why did I not notice that my hunger was gone before this? My thinking is slow—it is good that I am near wolf ridge and the end of my travel.

Lion Hunter looked up. Wolf Ridge, the distinctive gouge out of the white granite mountainside that Spirit Man described to him, was halfway up the mountainside. The sheer wall above him was too steep to climb, so Lion Hunter decided to continue on the elk trail until he came to a more favorable climbing place. Before him, the elk trail picked its way through a mass of boulders, debris deposited by the landslides from above.

His thoughts had drifted back to the strangeness of knowing he should be hungry and yet not being so when he was startled by a voice from nearby.

"Hey, ya, young Hunter. Do you speak to me?" Lion Hunter remained silent, brow furrowed as he rummaged through his memory for a reason someone might ask such a question of him when he had not been speaking.

"Ho, look at this young one, great Spirit Fathers," the voice said. "He brags he will soon be a warrior, yet does not even look around for danger when he is alone in the wilderness and hears a strange voice. A warrior? Ha."

Lion Hunter lifted his head, looked around and was stunned to find a raven standing on a boulder just beyond arm's reach. The animal stood silent, looking at him with the same intensity the ravens at the bear feast had while waiting near the two yearling carcasses.

"You are Coyote Spirit?" Lion Hunter asked the raven, his brow furrowed. "What danger could you be?" The raven cocked its head to the side then stretched its wings and lifted off the rock swooping out over the river valley in silence.

"That was a raven, foolish boy. I do not make myself visible because I do not wish to be seen with a boy who acts so senseless."

"You have come to taunt me like you did when the she-lion hunted me in the darkness two winters ago. Why do you do this?" Lion Hunter asked his question, not sure what direction he should be looking. There was only the day's silence around him.

Lion Hunter stopped walking and looked back, studying the trail behind, squinting his eyes to help his concentration. He saw no sign he was being followed.

He peered down over the edge of the drop-off and was shifting his attention back to the trail in front of him when sudden movement caught his eye. An eerie sensation shot through his body, like the startled flinch that follows unexpectedly walking into a spider web or … maybe like being stalked by a she-lion when you are alone in the dark. He tried to hold on to the sensation, using it to pull his disarrayed thoughts back into the real world.

More movement. His head jerked, eyes locking onto a chubby fur ball scurrying across the trail. It was a marmot, its mouth stuffed with a thick wad of grass. The animal was hurrying back to its burrow—a hole as big around as one of Lion Hunter's thighs tucked beneath a large uneven boulder that jutted out over part of the trail before him.

Lion Hunter stood, allowing his heart to slow. The dullness that had beset him throughout the rest of the day gradually returned, settling around him like a warm haze.

He sat down. He was considering what he should do next when he heard Spirit Man's words, drifting out of nothingness to settle in his thoughts.

"When you do not eat or drink, a strangeness comes into your heart. It will be hard to make your think-habit after you camp on the mountain. So," his mentor cautioned, "you must check for any sign of danger as soon as you come to the ridge. Then, when you are sure there is no threat, make your camp before anything else.

"As time passes," Spirit Man pressed, "your thinking will grow less clear."

"But Grandfather, why do I fast then?" Lion Hunter asked.

"Visions are like floating seeds blown from the dandelion, Hunter. They drift with every breeze, shifting and scattering quickly. Your heart must be ready in that one moment when your vision floats by whispering its secrets to you. Fasting opens the corners of your heart so this vision will find a place to become trapped in."

Lion Hunter turned back to the boulder-strewn elk path. Beyond the obstruction, the trail meandered along the base of the mountain, finally pinching out of sight around the curve of the mountain. He knew the elk trail would eventually turn up into the forest, but that was of no matter to him. Before going that far he determined to turn from the path and climb straight up the mountain to the ridge.

He chose a path through the rest of the boulder field and started walking.

Coyote Man's mockery, and the shock of the marmot experience afterward, teased at the edge of his thoughts as he picked a path through fractured chunks of granite. Those incidents were either premonition or part of the confusion Spirit Man warned him to expect, but he could not tell which.

He worked his way through the boulders just as the elk had before him, picking his speed up to a full walk as the sheer wall at his shoulder gradually gave way to an up-mountain slope that was still steep, but climbable. After briefly considering whether to begin his climb there, Lion Hunter decided to go on, hoping to find a gentler incline—one safer for someone in his weakened condition.

Instead, he came to a huge talus slide that covered the elk trail entirely for a distance he believed would probably take him the rest of the afternoon to cross. The vast cascade of rock stretched from far up the mountainside to where the mountain met the valley below. Although a few elk had carefully crossed the slide to pick up the trail beyond, Lion Hunter decided against attempting the walk and resolved to ascend the mountain at the edge of the slide.

Shortly after beginning his climb, he came across the first sign that a grizzly had also chosen this spot to ascend, paralleling the talus field.

This bear comes to hunt the night moths that sleep beneath the rocks higher up.

Like the grizzly, Lion Hunter knew that moths gathered in the high mountains each summer. They visited flowers at night and slept in nests of many thousands beneath talus formations during the day.

Lion Hunter saw hundreds of mini-slides where the bear had walked out onto the talus slope digging down into the rocks to feast upon the hordes of moths concealed there. He studied the ground beneath his feet more closely and soon found more evidence of the bear's passage—deep claw marks in the earth in one place, part of a print in another and, smelling it long before seeing it, a pile of the animal's scat. He scattered the pile, examining its insides for dryness and content and decided it was three days old. Comfortable the bear had hunted out the talus slide and moved on, Lion Hunter continued his climb.

As afternoon shadows settled on the other side of the valley, Lion Hunter climbed up onto the broad shelf of Wolf Ridge. A mature forest of lodgepole pine populated the slopes on either side of the flat shelf, but the plant life on here was far less stately.

Three stunted whitebarks grew out of the fractured rocks nearest the cliff wall, and a grassy meadow spread from their base to a point several strides from the edge of the cliff.

The meadow, an area not large enough to graze more than one pony, that is, if you could even get a pony to the ledge, gave way to a twisted mass of snowbrush that looked as if it would defy penetration.

Lion Hunter found a game trail that forced its way through the snowbrush and forced his way through to the drop-off's edge. Standing there, looking down over the fallen boulders below him, he recognized the area as the boulder field part of the elk trail he'd picked his way through earlier in the afternoon. He saw a dark spot scrambling across the path and remembered the marmot that had frightened him as he passed there.

You are un-cautious little one. And fat. I might eat you when I return after my vision quest.

He was surprised when he absently rubbed the back of his right arm and discovered a trail of blood oozing from elbow to fingertips.

Lion Hunter was finally on Wolf Ridge. The climb had been exhausting, and he did not feel like preparing his camp right then so he sat down at the edge of the cliff and closed his eyes, drinking in the fresh breeze that lifted up from the valley below.

Later, his exhaustion exaggerated by inaction, he climbed back to his feet and walked along the cliff's edge where he came to a second game trail, this one little larger than what a rabbit would need. Convinced it would be easier to force his way back through the snowbrush here, he headed for the back wall of the ledge. The strip of snowbrush was much narrower on the west end of the ledge and he worked through it in little time but, never the less, emerged with more scratches.

Once out on the grass again, he removed the sheepskin shirt from his pack and lay down using it as a pillow. The afternoon breeze drifted over his bare chest, carrying away the sweat accumulated during his climb. Lion Hunter was content.

As he relaxed, his thoughts drifted back to his wolf dream. In that dream, he'd first arrived on Wolf Ridge by crawling up over the cliff's edge. Now he knew that was impossible. The drop was too sheer.

He shifted his thoughts to the dream-wolf's startling eyes and the momentary fright they caused before the rest of its body materialized out of the surrounding granite wall. The creature was large, a grey-white male with black-tipped ears and surprisingly bold behavior. Lion Hunter knew wolves to be fearless in defense of themselves and their territory, but most of his experience found them wary of humans, slinking off upon first sight. The puzzle of his dream-wolf's behavior eluded him, so his thoughts drifted back to Spirit Man's admonition about camp preparation.

I lay down when I should be making a safe camp. What would my Willow say?

Lion Hunter shook away the cobwebs covering his thoughts and forced himself to rise and set his pack aside so he could explore unburdened.

Which direction? He looked around.

Wolf Ridge was flat, as though a great triangular chunk of the mountain had long ago been cut away from it by one of the ancient giants Pony Man told stories about. Farther up, beyond the ledge's steep cliff, the mountain's hump tapered off and remained both forested and gentle until it rose up beyond the tree line. The same was true of the forest both right and left of the ridge. The rock wall, where it had been sliced away from the mountain, rose up sharply, six times Lion Hunter's height in some places, and ancient fragments of bleached tree roots hung out of the earth high above, over the wall's edge.

While gazing at the wall, he noticed faint signs of a path ascending to a small cave opening three-quarters of the way up. In reckless haste, he decided to investigate the cavity before any further search for a campsite.

The first half of the path's incline was gentle, but the second half was sharper than he originally thought—it was more of a climb from rock-hold to rock-hold than walking a path. The actual cavity was little deeper than his arm's length but the dust on its floor had a few hairs and old cat prints in it.

This is a lay place for a small lion or a lynx. Probably lynx. There is always good rabbit hunting in lodgepole forests.

No longer interested in the cave, he turned around and stood looking down over the table of the ledge. Doing so he set one foot in front of the lay and the other on a crumbling vein of black rock protruding from the wall little more than the width of his foot. The brittle vein angled slightly downward and stretched several paces eastward of the cave as a narrow ledge. He looked over at the three whitebark pines he'd seen from the ledge's floor earlier—they were no more than a stone's throw away.

He thought of Spirit Man and his warning about the importance of preparing a camp.

Dark is coming.

Lion Hunter scrambled his way back down to the ledge, gouging an elbow on a sharp rock along the way. He turned, walking away from the direction of the talus slide, thinking it would be easier to find a suitable campsite just inside the forest on the undisturbed side of the ridge.

An unnoticed trail of blood trickled down the back of his arm.

17

Lion Hunter left the ridge and wandered into the towering lodgepole forest, his movements silent on its bed of fallen needles. Nearby, the forest floor was not flat enough to camp on comfortably, so he searched in a circle, not wanting, unless necessary, to stray far from the ridge he was leaving now that it was dark. He soon found a toppled sugar pine. Its roots were ripped out of the ground, leaving a large spot of exposed earth beneath.

This is a fine campsite. Flat and soft.

He plopped down into the dirt void left by the tipped-up roots. Tired and in need of rest, he was asleep in moments. Food did not enter his thoughts.

* * *

Lion Hunter opened his eyes and pulled himself up into a sitting position, squinting in the morning light. He stretched, then, midway into a leisurely yawn, remembered where he was. A pang of disappointment swept through him.

My vision has not yet come.

During his training, Spirit Man told him how unpredictable visions could be. "There is no way to know when they will come," the old man said. "Visions come when it is their time to come. A vision does not care for your wishes—it wants only to deliver its message in a time your heart will see."

Lion Hunter was disappointed despite the admonition.

He looked around to orient himself. Bright sunlight filtered through the trees. He decided that was the direction of the open ledge—the one he'd wandered away from last night without orienting himself. He exhaled—relieved to discover the ledge was still nearby. He felt ashamed for his failure. He was here for his vision quest to become a man, to prove his worth to his people and to learn the secrets of his future. This was a poor start.

Disappointed, he crossed his forearms, absently rubbing his upper arms with his hands as his thoughts began drifting again. He felt something odd and pulled his hand away to see what it was.

What is this dried blood?

He rolled his arm around for a look and found scraped and scabbed-over skin from elbow to shoulder. There were more scrapes and some blood on his legs.

Where did I get these wounds?

He knew that fasting and going without water would affect him physically, but he had not counted on losing memory of the things he did. Troubled, he looked around for his pack and was near alarm when he remembered leaving it at the foot of the cave trail before walking into the forest the night before.

I left my pack when I went to make camp. Again, I was careless. I must concentrate before I make decisions now—Grandfather would not be proud of me.

Lion Hunter climbed to his feet, took a moment to adjust to a minor wave of dizziness, and then walked back toward the ledge to collect his pack.

I am ashamed, Grandfather. I did not make my camp and check for danger last night, as I should have.

After retrieving his pack and returning to the fallen tree camp, Lion Hunter dug a small campfire pit and collected rocks to circle it with. He did not plan to use the fire pit, but if he needed one after having his vision it would be ready. The cold, when it came, was a thing all braves on vision quests endured—it was a trial of their spirits, one more burden to all who sought to claim the honor of manhood.

The fat marmot from the base of the cliff crept into his thoughts. He imagined its chubby little body roasting over orange-yellow flames, grease dripping and sizzling on the fire beneath it. The thought vanished and was replaced with the abrupt realization that his mouth was bone dry. He became irritated with himself for daydreaming again. Snatching up his pack, he stuffed it between the tree roots that were his camp's wind block and absentmindedly poked a few wads of pine needles in the space behind to conceal it.

He stood, then checked the surrounding ground for a small pebble to suck on. He needed saliva to comfort the thick dry wad his tongue had become since he quit drinking water.

He snatched one up and jammed it into his mouth—ashamed he hadn't done so earlier as he was taught.

Disturbed by his new round of remembered mistakes, he stomped off into the woods with no real plan. A blur of thoughts played out senseless experiences as he treaded along among the pine needles. He was moving carelessly, not paying attention to where he walked or, what dangers might be present when thoughts of his wolf dream came to him. Thinking about the wolf and what the holy man said the dream might have meant improved his mood. He stopped and carefully thought through his next move. He would look for wolf sign as he investigated this part of the forest for any danger that might be present, something he should have done before exploring the ridge yesterday afternoon.

Holding on to his resolution to find wolf sign, he checked knee-high bushes for the animal's hair, carefully sniffed likely marking spots at trail crossings, and scanned all animal trails for prints and scat. Concentrating on his search for wolf sign made him feel better than he had for the last two days. He was just beginning to feel the joy of the hunt when he smelled human urine.

Lion Hunter stopped dead, carefully darting his eyes in every direction before daring to move again. He slowly backed up a step, scanning the area surrounding him, sniffing. The source of the scent was in the needles at the base of the tree nearest to where he now stood. The needles were disturbed, moved, their stems uniformly aligned in one direction while floating the short distance the unknown person's urine stream had carried them. He sniffed the tree's bark—the smell became heaviest at the same height Lion Hunter knew it would if he relieved himself there.

So, stranger, you are a man and my height.

Heart pounding, he carefully inspected the surrounding forest floor. He'd been moving across the top of the mountain's hump, paying no attention to the possible danger signs he was supposed to be looking for.

First, he needed to know how long ago the human passed. The tree's bark was still dark where the urine had splashed over it but no longer shined with surface wetness.

This morning, then. While I slept.

He stood up straight, carefully looking in every direction for the telltale outline of a human, any form that conflicted with the randomness of surrounding bushes and trees.

He returned his attention to the forest floor, carefully studying the surroundings. Behind were the signs left by his careless wandering. Shame flushed over him briefly as he continued his effort to determine the direction the stranger moved after leaving the tree. Three strides away he spotted a group of pine needles pushed up into the shape of a moccasin toe. He imagined the length of a stride and shifted his eyes backward along the line between the toe sign and tree he stood beside. He found another disturbance where he expected, then the final one, the step closest to him.

We travel in the same direction. I must concentrate and make very good decisions.

He took a deep breath, and looked back over his shoulder at the evidence of his own passage while he'd been looking for wolf sign. Another flush. He bit his lip. Before moving he looked around again just in case the other man was nearby, watching.

His pack was concealed, but the disturbance left by his carelessness could lead the intruder directly back to his campsite. Sudden alarm swept through him.

Did he stand over me as I slept? Lion Hunter felt as if he'd been kicked in the stomach.

He knew no others from his band were on vision quest, and he was sure no Wolf Ridge hunters would come to the sacred mountain to kill. Cramping, from the imagined kick, crept up into his chest. He spun and hurried back to the tree where the danger of a stranger's presence first revealed itself to him.

Avoiding the clutter of his own back trail, he quickly examined each of the other directions the intruder could have come from and was rewarded with the discovery of a series of disturbances coming down from farther up the mountainside. He leaned against the tree heavily, head cradled in the crook of his arm. The stranger was as uncaring of the sign he left behind as he was.

Thank you Spirit Fathers for watching over me. I will honor you with all my doings from this time on.

Lion Hunter stood up, took a deep breath, and settled himself. He looked first at the stranger's back trail, then beyond the tree to the toe cup disturbance while concentrating on using his think-habit.

The stranger is not one of my people. He does not walk carefully. I know he did not see my camp otherwise he would be more careful. That is good, he believes he is alone and has no fear. That is good also.

Lion Hunter relaxed a little—still, there was danger. He needed to know what the stranger's purpose was.

This place is the center of Wolf Ridge territory, but you are not one of my people. You do not come here to raid—there are none here to raid. You do not cut lodge poles or hunt… the journey here is too far for those things.

Lion Hunter's thoughts began to dim so he bent, sniffed again at the tree bark, and let the stranger's spoor sharpen his senses with purpose.

You are not a trader—too far away from those to trade with.

He pinched his brow together, considering the reasons why someone might travel this far up the side of a mountain rather than on more level ground.

Who then? A wanderer? One who cautiously scouts the land before continuing on your journey? But you are not cautious, and there was none of your sign on the ridge where you would have looked out over the elk trail and beyond.

He decided he needed to have more information.

If I follow your back-trail, I will be safe because you are not there. Will I learn anything? Possibly, but then I will not know where you are.

Lion Hunter again cautioned himself to remain alert. He looked along the line of foot disturbances he could see to decide where the stranger might be going.

Your direction will bring you to the scree-slide. Maybe you look to use it for a quick descent, and I will not have to worry about you anymore. The grizzly might surprise you.

Lion Hunter smiled at the thought. He was not worried that the trail he left behind during his ascent would be found, no one would climb down a steep mountain when they could fast step in a scree and get to the bottom so much easier and quicker.

He chose to follow the stranger.

* * *

The stranger passed up the scree-slide and continued traversing the mountain. That surprised Lion Hunter, but he continued following, still concerned about the man's presence on the mountain. Lion Hunter passed several mountain snowberry bushes before noticing that none of the berries had been picked. The stranger was not eating, but hunters always eat when possible. He scratched his head and tried to organize his thoughts.

Then he saw the campsite.

Lion Hunter instantly dropped to his belly and crawled beneath some snow bush, pressing his way forward until he could safely peer through its remaining crown to study the scene before him. His heart thumped in his chest. He was within full view of the camp before realizing how exposed he was. His sloppiness was a huge worry. He silently cursed the need for fasting, desperate to excuse his failure.

You have a camp? You are careless and you wander around with no purpose? Who are you that you stay on our sacred mountain and feel no danger?

He studied the empty camp. A pack sat on the ground propped up against a fallen log, a lance leaning next to it. Wild flowers in the surrounding flat were trampled.

Lion Hunter could smell fresh burnt charcoal and decided the stranger used the log as a firebreak. The fire pit would be on its other side.

Why do you not smother your ashes with dirt? You do not know about the grizzly or you would not be so careless. If he is still near he will smell your coals and return to investigate.

Lion Hunter remained hidden, watching the camp for any movement. He did not want to take the chance the stranger was sleeping nearby.

His eyes closed and he fell asleep.

Suddenly he heard the sound of movement behind him. When there was no attack, he slowly turned his head as far as he could and looked out the extreme side of one eye. Three cow elk stood unmoving several strides away staring directly at the bush he lay beneath. A first year calf idled nearby, freshly cropped grass dangling from its chomping mouth.

Ahh, thank you my brothers. You smell me, yes, but you also tell me that no others creep up behind me.

Lion Hunter knew as long as he did not move the big deer would not sense threat. Just the same, they were aware of his presence. He watched as the three adults raised and turned their heads sampling the breeze with flared nostrils. They were checking for other scents coming up from the lowlands beyond the camp. Brief moments later, they returned to sampling his scent and he knew they had found nothing else to interest them. Reassured, he let them move off without moving himself so that he could see which direction they chose. That was a safe direction to travel.

Confident no one was near the camp, he crawled out of the bushes and walked up to it. A glance at the lance assured him it was not so well crafted as were weapons his people made. He studied the pack. The workings and decoration of it was the same fine quality as were Spirit Man's shirt and moccasins. His mother, a Crow, made them for him. She was the only member of his band that produced such fine leatherwork, but she was gone months now. Besides, he was not following a woman.

This was a Crow camp.

All who traveled the Northern Plains needed and carried much the same things to aid in their survival. Lion Hunter did not think to inspect the pack contents besides, he now believed he was following a boy like himself, not a warrior. He did not understand why a Crow would come to this holy mountain.

His mood changed abruptly. Discovering that he and a Crow brave had come to the same mountain made him feel giddy, oddly, even safer, after all his morning fears. He sat contemplating his situation. He decided the Crow was on his vision quest.

Even this careless Crow boy will sometime discover my sign. I think I will find and watch him first.

The trail leaving the camp was fresher than that he followed in the morning. The Crow spent some time resting before leaving again. This new trail went downhill, then doubled back paralleling, but not using the path both boys used that morning. Lion Hunter knew he was close behind the Crow, and his senses were keyed. He crept along behind his unseen quarry, passing the top of the scree slide before arriving at the rock edge looking down over the broad ledge of Wolf Ridge.

There was lots of disturbance here. Sign that the Crow crawled up to the rock edge, laid down, and watched the ledge below before continuing on.

Lion Hunter filled his lungs with a huge draught of the air tumbling up over the ledge below. He held it for a moment, hoping to clear his thoughts. There was a trace scent, something in the air that tickled at the edges of his awareness, but he had to let it go. In this moment caution was his greatest concern.

He was thinking about his next move when a flash of movement from below, at the far corner of the ledge, caught his attention He wasn't sure exactly where, amongst all the bushes, the movement had occurred, so he waited, defocusing his eyes, scanning the whole end of the ledge for any additional movement.

His attention had just begun to drift when the movement occurred again. This time, he felt sure he knew which bush it was in. He shook his head clear and concentrated on the bush, searching out background lines that did not match the random limbs of the bush itself.

The warm afternoon sun began baking his uncovered torso and head, and sweat soon began trickling down from his brow. He was rubbing the side of his brow on the arm cushioning his face from the ground when, through the leaves of the bushes, he puzzled out the shape of a pack and a hand holding its strap.

It was his pack, he realized with absolute certainty.

You steal my pack? For this one small coup you will suffer much defeat, Crow boy. Lion Hunter's hand crept down to the hilt of his knife, fingers gripping its heft as he lay seething.

So, why do you now crawl like a snake through the bushes of Wolf Ridge?

Another bead of sweat coursed its way down through one eyebrow and rolled into his eye. He blinked away the sting, continuing his watch, trying to understand the Crow's intensions.

Understanding abruptly replaced his thoughts of revenge … the Crow was carefully paralleling Lion Hunter's own path, the one made while he returned to the ridge to collect that same pack this morning.

I walked this path three times. Does he track so poorly he did not see the other tracks leaving my camp? He thinks I am still on the ridge. Hiding in the bushes? Ha!

Lion Hunter's eyes swept over to the lynx cave and its precipitous approach.

If I hurry I can get to the cave entrance from the opposite direction before he is able to see my climb.

Mind racing with anticipated glee, Lion Hunter backed away from the rocky overlook. Once out of sight, he leapt to his feet and raced back to the scree-slide then scrambled down the bear path beside it—he didn't want to chance the noise of using the scree itself. Once parallel to the ridge, he ran softly along its path to the base of the rock wall.

Lion Hunter carefully scaled the sharp incline leading to the cave, certain the Crow could not detect him. A smile pulled at the corners of his mouth as he sat down cross legged on the tiny perch before the cave—resolved to make no movement so the Crow's eye would not be attracted overhead to where he sat in full view. The whitebark pine crowns stuck out far it concealed his presence and would continue to do so for a little longer as the Crow wormed his way through the thick brush. Lion Hunter was confident the Crow boy would be too busy examining the trail and remaining silent to look up and see him.

Lion Hunter tingled with excitement when the Crow came into view, but after a short time somberly conceded to himself that the boy's stealth was superb—only rarely did a leaf twitch and, for all his progress, no single sound drifted up from below.

Lion Hunter's first plan was to wait until the Crow crawled to the rock wall beneath the cave then heap mockery on him from above. Now he was not so sure. Maybe he would just call out to him and make trade-talk—pretend he had the Crow's pack to trade for his own, and then see what happened.

He was still pondering how he might initiate contact when an abrupt burst of movement jerked his attention back to the scene below.

The Crow was standing bolt upright with a horrified look on his face. Three paces away a sleepy-eyed boar grizzly had its head poked up out of the bushes staring at him. A jolt of fear for the Crow shot through Lion Hunter's body and without thinking he leapt to his feet. The stupefied bear now up on all fours, snapped its head sideways focusing on Lion Hunter, and instantly became fully alert.

Lion Hunter froze, immobilized with fear, this time for himself.

The Crow scrambled away from the bear, arms and legs whirling madly as he crashed through the thick brush trying to make good his escape. The bear jerked his head back and forth between the two boys twice more, then burst into action.

18

Letting out a thunderous bawl, the bear launched itself after the fleeing Crow. Lion Hunter looked on helpless, as the boy's meager head start shrank with alarming swiftness. A final bound over rock debris strewn about the base of the nearest whitebark allowed the Crow to leap up into the tree.

The grizzly's delayed start let the young Crow get just high enough to avoid its first brutal swipe. Its finger-long claws raked across the tree's trunk, sending splintered wood exploding into the air.

The full weight of the animal's fat-laden body came down on the other front paw as the bear's momentum slung it past the tree. The paw knifed into a mound of weather-splintered rock at the base of the cliff. Lion Hunter saw the animal wince with pain.

Rebounding from the rock wall, the raging animal raced back to the tree and hurled itself upward, one giant paw wrapped around the trunk while the second shot out to snag the scrambling Crow's foot. Instead, it hooked one of his moccasins and the monstrous bear slid back down the slim grey-white trunk amid flying bark and cracking tree limbs.

Lion Hunter looked down on the scene helplessly as the Crow scrambled to the uppermost limbs of the stunted tree and seized hold of its shrinking trunk with both arms and legs. The tree was rooted in a thin layer of soil clinging to the cliff's rocks. It was so deprived of adequate nutrients it was neither tall enough nor thick enough to withstand the onslaught of a large, angry grizzly.

Regaining its balance, the bear glowered up at the Crow. Saliva spewed from its gaping mouth as it panted, and its massive ribcage heaved with his climbing effort.

"Hey you, great bear," Lion Hunter hollered out instinctively, surprising even himself. "Are you so cowardly you chase a boy instead of another angry bear?"

Still hugging the tree's limbs, the Crow spun his head around and looked up at Lion Hunter, his face registering a new astonishment.

The grizzly stared at the trembling Crow a moment longer then swiveled its eyes over to Lion Hunter. There was little immediate interest in the creature's look, but the boy noticed its eyes shift to the path leading up to the cave before returning its full attention to the Crow.

Still panting, the bear lifted its paw. A gapping, gushing wound poured blood out onto the rocky ground. Even from his position thirty strides or more up the cliff side, Lion Hunter could see the huge jagged tear in the paw's flesh. The animal licked at the wound absently while continuing to stare up at the Crow in his undersized place of refuge.

The bear abruptly lifted itself up onto its hind legs, leaning both forefeet against the tree. Still looking up, it stretched its foreleg up toward the Crow, but its menacing, claws were still three branches away from hooking its prey.

The grizzly shifted its weight back and forth getting good footing, then, placing both forefeet on the trunk, began bouncing its bulk against the tree. Each jolt shook the tree with such violence the Crow jarred from one branch to another, barely managing to keep himself out of the grizzly's reach.

Initially the tree withstood the violent onslaught, recoiling back to a quivering upright position after each blow. But the whitebark was poorly rooted and, eventually, it tilted so far backward it came to rest against the cliff wall.

The bear, unable to knock the tree farther over, shuffled around to the side and continued its assault on the tree's trunk. The whitebark slid sideways along the cliff wall while the terror-stricken Crow clutched desperately at fissures in the rock wall—his legs still wrapped around the tree.

Fist-sized chunks of granite had peeled from the granite wall and lay scattered near the cave entrance. Lion Hunter grabbed two.

His first heave was so powerful his forward momentum nearly toppled him from the ledge. As Lion Hunter tottered on the ledge, the chunk of rock struck the animal's shoulder with a thud, so loud the Crow looked up to see where it came from. But the blow went unnoticed by the bear as it continued its violent assault on the tree. The whitebark sagged, scraping ever further along the granite wall—dangerously close to toppling over on its side.

The second rock, thrown with all of his rabbit hunting skills, struck the bear on the muzzle beneath its left eye. Lion Hunter heard the crunch of its impact. The beast dropped back to all fours, shaking its head.

"Ha. You, smelly bear, you have no sense. You attack two warriors who…" the bear turned and fixed him with a malevolent look.

Aiiiee, he is going to attack me.

Panic struck Lion Hunter's heart. He frantically looked for someplace safe, anyplace. He was trapped standing on a narrow shelf, clinging to a rock wall.

The enormous animal's next reaction was terrifyingly quick. It spun and launched itself at a full run across the meadow. It was half way up the trail and nearing the steep part of the climb to the cave before Lion Hunter recovered enough from his fear to take action.

Just as the enraged bear clawed its way up and over the remaining precipitous incline, Lion Hunter remembered the narrow black-rock vein jutting out from the cliff wall next to the cave. He scrambled out onto its narrow shelf, fingertips clutching fractures in the cliff's wall, and the balls of his feet dangerously balanced on the vein's crumbling edge. He crabbed along the vein so quickly he lost his footing and dangled until once again finding purchase for first one toe, then a whole foot, and finally, both feet. He glanced down, legs shaking. The drop was four times his height, but a fall from that height wasn't the real danger. The bear could scamper back down and reach him long before he could recover from the fall.

The scrambling bear reached the flat terrace in front of the cave but had to bunch all four feet together in the lynx-sized space. It stood there teetering, glaring at Lion Hunter, huffing from the effort of its climb.

There was less space between them than the spread of Lion Hunter's outstretched arms. This close, the boy could smell the grizzly's rank odor and remembered with sudden clarity the trace scent he detected and dismissed earlier, while spying down at the Crow from the cliff edge above. Absurdly, Lion Hunter remembered the advice Spirit Man had given him at the scene of the bear killings. 'Memorize this grizzly stink, Hunter. They are shrewd and dangerous. Remembering could save your life one day.'

My fasting is too long and my thoughts soft. This bear will kill me if I do not use my think-habit.

The animal pressed its shoulder against the rock, counter-balancing as it slid its mass along the rock wall until it had a clear view across the short distance between them. Lion Hunter jerked his senses back to the present, gathering his courage and pushing back against a swelling sense of impending death.

The animal's small black eyes intelligently searched the surrounding rocks for a better foothold, a way to balance its massive body so it could reach out and hook Lion Hunter from the wall. Lion Hunter's feet were trembling more violently now, their strength waning, ready to give way at any moment. He moved one foot, and found a small improvement but was too frightened to attempt the same with the other foot.

"I am a warrior, you smelly bear," he shouted—his chin now quivering in sync with the rest of his body.

In reply the bear lifted up on its rear legs, chest pressed against the rock wall and front limbs stretched wide as it balanced trying to avoid toppling backward from the incline. The grizzly was nearly twice as tall as Lion Hunter, its monstrous head now stretched out so far toward him he could feel the heat of its breath as it looked down at him.

Fear-frozen, Lion Hunter clung to the wall while the grizzly's claws scratched and clicked against the rock, ever nearer. Dark blood leaked from its paw, smearing the white rock face, dribbling red runnels down the craggy wall surface. The bear's menacing nearness triggered raw mental images in Lion Hunter of his own blood splattered against the wall.

Fatigue set off a series of quivers that raced through him as panic began flooding his thoughts.

The grizzly kept coming, shifting its weight and moving a rear foot out onto the rock vein. It rebalanced, carefully leaned its head in Lion Hunter's direction, and slid its terrifying forepaw closer. The bear's claws were within an arm's length now and Lion Hunter's mind raced, but all reason had escaped him.

"Aiiiieee!" erupted the Crow from across the meadow. The bear's eyes slid toward him, then back at Lion Hunter, then back to the Crow again. Drool strung from its loose hanging lips and hot panting waves of foul bear-breath washed over Lion Hunter's terror.

Tearing his own eyes away from the bear, Lion Hunter looked sideways at the Crow and was thunderstruck to discover him balanced on the rocks beneath the tree. The young man was beating two large chunks of rock together with loud 'clacking' sounds, screaming at the bear in his own language.

When the bear did not take his bait, the Crow jumped down to the grass clearing and edged out into the open, still pounding his rocks together and screaming defiantly. The bear hesitated, looking back and forth between the two.

Lion Hunter watched the animal's weight shift as its muscles bunched. Preparing to move, it nearly lost its balance, then jerked its rear foot back to the flat terrace in front of the lynx cave. Before committing farther, it looked back at Lion Hunter, calculating, then again back to the Crow, who now shuffled even farther into the clearing—away from the meager safety of his whitebark refuge.

Apparently deciding the Crow was easier prey, the bear slid its upper body slowly down the wall until all four of its feet were once again on the tiny shelf. After a final look in Lion Hunter's direction, the bear turned its full attention to the Crow. As it stared down at him, the muscles of its shoulder twitched, and it began rocking from one foot to another, expressing its angry frustration in silent body motion. Finally, decision made, the animal backed its immense haunches back down over the first boulder on the steep portion of the path. That is when the Crow began hurling rocks.

Rock after rock rained down on the animal's body as it backed warily down the steep drop, flinching and recoiling under the Crow's barrage. When the bear's hindquarters hung suspended seeking a new purchase, a single paw, the injured one, held its weight. At that moment, a rock crashed down on its exposed toes and, bawling in pain, the bear yanked his injured paw free of the rock. Grip lost, the bear's immense body launched into a jolting backward-belly-slide down over the rough rocks until it finally came to a crashing halt on the lower part of the path.

Immediately springing to its feet, the furious bear raced down the remaining incline where it launched itself out onto the meadow. By that time, the retreating Crow was well up into the tree.

Lion Hunter, muscles at their limit, had edged back off of the black-rock vein and onto the cave's flat terrace during the bear's descent. Fingers numb and legs still quivering, he bent, scooped up two more rocks and turned back to launch another attack in defense of the Crow.

Surprisingly, the bear was not attacking. It had stopped in the clearing and was looking up at the Crow. Lion Hunter sensed the bear's frustration and felt a flood of elation.

Barely able to contain himself, Lion Hunter looked over at the Crow only to see a new astonishment flood into the young man's facial expression. He was not looking at the bear.

Lion Hunter followed the other's eyes. In front of the brambles, near the game trail Lion Hunter had taken when forcing his way to the ledge's drop-off, a large grey-white wolf with black-tipped ears stood motionless, its yellow-green eyes fixed on the bear.

The wolf of my dream! Joy erupted within Lion Hunter.

The bear, facing the other way, did not know the wolf was there. The panting grizzly had been looking at the Crow also. It turned its head back and looked at Lion Hunter. Its black eyes lingered a moment, swiveled back to the Crow, then glanced back over its own shoulder. Upon seeing the wolf, the startled bear spun so quickly it stumbled sideways, but its legs never stopped moving.

For a single breath the grizzly burst into frantic retreat but in its next breath surprise-fear gave way to a fearsome rage and the bear launched into a violent tantrum. The outraged bear uprooted great masses of earth with blow after blow—dirt and grass flew everywhere in chaotic confusion. The bear's body rippled with the violence of its contortions. It bellowed and thrashed, venting its anger until, abruptly, the massive grizzly stopped and with breath-stealing malevolence swung its massive head around to face the wolf. Death resided in its hunched stance.

Ha! You are ashamed because you are seven times bigger than this wolf and you ran like a coward.

Ears back and hackles raised, the grizzly shuffled sideways toward the wolf—exposing its immense profile, bristling with terrifying silence. The air was filled with the stench of the creature.

Lion Hunter shivered as he watched the bear sidestep toward *his* wolf.

The wolf stood at its full height, bright eyes measuring the approaching bear. It showed no hint of intimidation.

The grizzly launched an attack. When its blows found only brambles, the bear spun, eyes tracking—what its muscles could not—the wolf which so nimbly evaded its attack—scrambled briefly then trotted to the middle of the clearing.

The Crow yipped in celebration and Lion Hunter's own cheers quickly followed.

Once beyond the bear's reach, the wolf stopped and looked up, favoring both Indians with a pleased look before turning back to face the bear.

This time the wolf dipped its chest to the ground and stretched its paws out before it, pink tongue lolling from the side of its open mouth.

My wolf plays with this grizzly!

As the bear stood panting, it favored its injured paw, twice placing weight on it and flinching both times.

The grizzly launched its second attack, its immense body moving so quickly Lion Hunter saw only a blur. But the wolf slipped away from this second attack also, smoothly shifting from scrambling evasion to a light trot before it returned to the same spot where it first appeared in front of the brambles.

After catching its balance, the monster bear whirled to face the wolf a third time. Blood poured from its torn paw, saturating the grass beneath it, but now, the injury went unheeded. The bear's rage was checked, and its deliberate approach posed a different, more deadly, threat to the wolf.

The wolf's posture was different also. Now, with its mane erect and fangs bared, it snarled defiance at the grizzly.

Lion Hunter looked on in disbelief. A single wolf fighting a grizzly was beyond foolish.

Why do you do this, wolf? Flee while you live.

The grizzly launched its third attack with lightning speed, its great body rippling with the violence of its surge. Alarmed, Lion Hunter watched the wolf hold its ground until the last moment before scurrying sideways—away from the grizzly's good paw. The bear stretched out, swiping at the retreating wolf while planting all of its weight on the damaged paw. It flinched at contact with the ground, and the charge's momentum drove the bear's immense bulk forward until it crashed into the thick tangle of snowbrush. The brush, just tall enough to sweep the bear's legs from beneath its body, caused it to tumble, pitching and summersaulting until its heavy hindquarters launched out over the cliff's edge.

The shocked creature summoned all its strength in a momentous battle with gravity. Its giant claws dug into earth and bramble alike, ripping huge chunks of both from the floor of the ledge, but it was too late. Its massive weight prevailed and gradually, despite its courageous effort to cling to the safety of the ledge, it slipped farther and farther over the cliff's edge. In the end, only the sound of its hind feet clawing at the sheer rock wall could be heard as it clung to a last desperate hold on the claw-shredded earth of the ledge. Lion Hunter found himself looking into the shocked eyes of the grizzly with sadness. Moments later, the sickening sound of the creature smashing into the rocks far below penetrated the lingering silence and as quickly as terrifying danger had arrived, it was gone.

For a shocked moment, Lion Hunter stood, his heart still pounding. Then, he remembered the wolf.

His eyes found it sniffing at the ripped up earth near the cliff's edge. Lion Hunter glanced toward the tree just as the Crow's eyes found him. Both smiled and turned back to the wolf.

Finished smelling, the wolf raised its leg and scented an uprooted snowberry bush.

Done, it bunched its haunches and cleared the remaining snowberry bushes with a single leap.

Tongue lolling, the wolf sat and looked up at Lion Hunter with utter calmness in its expression. For a moment, Lion Hunter thought it might speak to him, just as Coyote Man had two years ago. But it did not.

Lion Hunter was still holding his breath when the wolf rose again, paused, in a three-legged stance to scratch at its shoulder, then trotted toward the east end of the ridge and disappeared into the shadows of the forest.

Still in the crown of his whitebark pine, the Crow repositioned himself to free his hands and turned to Lion Hunter. He signed.

"Question. Spirit wolf?"

Lion Hunter smiled broadly at the thought.

This wolf is my totem. My quest is over. I am a man now.

Elated, he signed back to the Crow.

"Yes. Maybe. You big hunter," he added, congratulating the Crow for saving his life.

The Crow smiled.

"You. Big hunter. Like me," he signed back.

"Bear. Not like, eat me. Better, jump over cliff," Lion Hunter suggested in jest.

"You save me. I save you. Good medicine." The Crow shifted in his perch, nearly losing his balance.

Lion Hunter nodded, taking a deep breath and letting it out slowly to calm himself.

After a moment he pointed toward the ground and both descended to the meadow where they continued their sign conversation while making their way to the drop-off to look for the bear.

From the edge, they looked down over the boulder field where Lion Hunter had watched the marmot the day before. The ruined body of the bear was there, well up-slope and off trail. There was no doubt it was dead.

"Wolf?" Lion Hunter signed and both began searching for anything that might prove the animal had been real.

Much later both returned to the meadow and sat, their disappointment evident. Neither found any sign of the animal that saved them. Lion Hunter decided the wolf was truly his vision. He turned to the Crow.

"Lion Hunter," he announced pointing to his own chest.

"Fox," the Crow responded, doing the same. The Crow looked to be about two years older than him.

"Fox," Lion Hunter said out loud, then signed, "much brave. Question. We brothers now?" He was asking if, now that each had saved the other, they would be friends.

The Crow smiled and made the *brother* sign. Lion Hunter smiled back, doing the same.

They retrieved Lion Hunter's pack from the brambles where Fox had left it so abruptly upon discovering the sleeping bear, then hiked in silence back up to the Crow's camp where they stopped to collect his belongs.

Taking a water bladder from his pack the Crow held it out to Lion Hunter, offering him a drink.

He hadn't had a drink for days. Remembering that he'd decided his quest was complete—Lion Hunter took the bag and lifted it to his mouth. He took in a small amount—allowed it to sting its way past his lips but then almost choked because his throat was so dry he couldn't swallow. After coughing hoarsely, he took in a tiny bit more and let it sit in his mouth a while before swallowing, this time, more carefully. The Crow watched.

"Question. You, quest?" the Crow asked, then waited for his new friend to nod before acknowledging the response with a nod of his own.

He lifted a cake of pemmican from a pocket in his shirt and laid it on a rock next to Lion Hunter before continuing their conversation.

Fox told Lion Hunter that he was a member of Chief High Elk's band. High Elk was renowned as a Warrior Chief of the Crow nation. He was famous for his bravery among most Northern Plains tribes.

Fox's band was the same one Lion Hunter's mother had been taken captive from.

"I, quest two years, before time," Fox signed.

You are eighteen and already a man. But if you are not here on a quest why are you here? And why did you not eat berries on the trail as others would?

When Lion Hunter asked about the berries, Fox laughed, replying that he was not hungry. The answer bothered Lion Hunter because at the time he'd been proud of himself for using his think-habit in deciding the Crow was also on his quest.

My thoughts fooled me because I was fasting.

Lion Hunter asked why his new friend was here, and Fox explained that his journey to White Mountain was to trade for black-rock arrow points.

"You, trader Indian?" Lion Hunter had met only a hand full of traders in his life. Traders did not often come into Wolf Ridge villages. More frequently, parties of warriors met with them at known trading sites on the open plain or went to their permanent villages where their people lived in family-sized mud lodges and grew tobacco and squashes.

In response to Lion Hunter's confused look, Fox smiled and told him he was not a trader himself, he was apprentice to his village's holy man and made the trip for him. His mentor, he told Lion Hunter, often traded tobacco for black-rock points with a strange old man who lived alone in the wilderness—a man that spoke the Crow tongue and wore Crow clothing but who was not Crow.

Lion Hunter sat straight up remembering the black-rock that Spirit Man collected from the boiling mud land they visited.

After considering this for a moment it also occurred to him that many of his people laughed at Pony Man, the storyteller and point maker, who made so many points before he was satisfied with those few he actually agreed to trade to his own people. They joked that he was too particular and that was why he had never taken a wife.

The Crow, making his point, poured many points out onto the ground from his pack. Lion Hunter smiled to himself, happy to know these new secrets about both Spirit Man and Pony Man.

It was time for him to travel back to his village—a man.

19

Fox and Lion Hunter spent the rest of that day and night together learning about each other and strengthening their 'brotherhood' bonds.

In the morning, Fox bid his new brother goodbye and set out to return to his village. He left a supply of pemmican and a spare water bladder behind, and, like a concerned older brother, suggested that Lion Hunter linger a few days until his health returned before beginning the return to his own village.

By the next morning Lion Hunter was taking in water at a normal rate and had eaten all of the pemmican left by Fox and some berries from nearby bushes. He was still not as steady or strong as he wanted to be, but he was anxious to return to his people as a new man. He decided to begin his home journey that day.

Lion Hunter walked back to the talus slide and looked down shaking his head. Side-jumping down on the slide would be quick, but he was still weak, and if he fell he could get hurt. He took the same bordering path he came upon two days before.

At the path's intersection with the elk trail, he turned toward the boulder field and began trudging along on his homeward journey.

His senses were still blunted. When he remembered to, he pinched himself or shook his head to clear away the muddle of random thoughts. Men on journeys often used elk trails, and he did not want to meet a stranger while in his present condition.

Turkey vultures were drifting in from all directions. Two circled overhead and now and again he caught glimpses of several others perched on rocks at the bottom of the cliff. He decided finding the bear's carcass would be simple.

A bearskin would be nice to lie back on in my lean-to.

He became excited, imagining himself arriving at his village with a fine talisman from the bear, something to brag about.

Bear thoughts lingering in his mind, he picked out a boulder near the trail that was taller than those surrounding it. He crawled to its top, climbed to his feet, and balanced himself carefully. He looked for the easiest route from the path to the carcass.

The deep brown color of the bear's coat contrasted starkly with the surrounding light color of the boulder field—that and the distinctive black shapes of stoop-necked vultures. He decided to leave the trail from where he was.

Making his way through the litter of fallen rocks was going to be challenging—it would be even worse trying to carry a heavy bear pelt back. He decided he might reconsider skinning the bear when he got there. It might be too much for him in his current state of weakness.

Reaching the carcass was more difficult than he thought it would be. He slipped and fell several times. The skin on his knee ripped open during one of the falls. Blood from the wound bled down his leg and into his moccasin.

Another fall left him lodged between two boulders, and he had to lie there for a while waiting for his resolve to return before continuing.

It was easy enough shooing away the only vulture that was feeding, but the flies were so thick he was reluctant to even approach. He sat down and examined the dead creature from a distance. Its coat was still thin and in poor condition from summer. Its head sustained a terrible blow and was so misshapen the skull, and even the teeth, would serve poorly as a trophy. In the end, he decided to take its claws—they could be fashioned into a necklace and would be easy to carry. He took a deep breath and waded in among the swarming flies.

Lion Hunter was able to cut off the foreparts of three of the animal's feet. The last foot was wedged beneath the weight of its carcass, and he could not budge its dead weight with what little strength he had left. He resolved to carve the claws away from flesh and cartilage of the feet later—somewhere the flies were not crawling in and out of his ears and nostrils.

When finished, he stuffed the bear's feet in his pack and wiped his knife clean on the bear's ratty fur. The meat was already turning and, though in need of rest, he wanted to put some distance between himself and the reeking carcass before sitting down and relaxing.

I will never again forget the stench of bear.

He crawled over several boulders moving downwind and in the general direction of the elk trail. Once out of range of both flies and stink, he sat and stared back toward the carcass.

He watched as one vulture hopped over to the carcass and began feeding. He pondered why none of the many others that gathered nearby joined the feed.

Is the meat not turned enough for your fine tastes?

He laughed at his own joke, the first humor he'd felt in days. Shortly, though, he began wondering again. He felt the vultures' behavior was very odd given all he knew about other wild creatures.

Two scrapes and an ankle twist later he made it back to the elk trail. He sat again, on a low rock alongside the trail this time. While resting, he took a long drought of water from the skin Fox left him and daydreamed he was licking duck grease from his fingers after a delicious eating binge. His stomach was getting better, but he was still exhausted.

Dull-eyed, Lion Hunter looked eastward along the trail. A few steps away, the marmot scurried across the trail just as it had when Lion Hunter first arrived at the mountain. He was so exhausted he hadn't even realized he was near the marmot hole. He smiled, letting his eyes close. His head nodded, jerked up, then nodded again as he leaned back against the rock behind him and drifted off.

"Yip, yip, yip. Aieeeeee!" The alarming war cry pierced his sleep, jerking him to nerve tingling wakefulness. He felt the thunderous pounding of horse hooves from the ground before even discovering which direction the attack was coming from.

Lion Hunter leaped to his feet, overbalanced, then pushed away from the nearest boulder while spinning to face his unknown attacker. His adversary came into focus as Lion Hunter reached for the knife at his belt, his only weapon.

Both warrior and mount bore down on him from the east. The ferocious-looking warrior, screaming a heart-chilling war cry, strained forward over his pony's out-stretched neck, war club in hand. Lion Hunter stood in the middle of the narrow trail, thoughts reeling.

The remembered image of the black-heart Blackfeet warrior diving aside to avoid Kills-In-The-Dark's charging pony flashed through Lion Hunter's mind.

Lion Hunter bunched his legs to leap just as a scurrying ball of fur squirted out onto the trail beneath the charging horse's feet. The startled horse jerked sideways, collided with a jutting boulder, then careened to the opposite side of the trail where it shouldered off a second boulder and crashed into Lion Hunter—all before the young man's impaired senses could command his body to leap aside. The force of the blow tumbled Lion Hunter over the edge of the path, sent his knife flying, and crushed the air from his lungs.

He landed sprawled over a pile of rocks, looking down on the valley far below, struggling to catch his breath. He was in serious danger and needed to get to his feet, to mount a defense, but he couldn't breathe. He was near panic when his stunned chest muscles finally began to respond.

Rocks were the only weapons available. He grabbed one up as air began wheezing back into his lungs. There was a flat area near the trail just above him. He dragged himself to his hands and knees and clawed his way back up to it prepared to stand and defend himself. Eyes darting, he caught the pony's nervous movement farther down the trail. The creature looked back still shaken by its recent panic. There was no sign of the warrior.

With enormous effort Lion Hunter staggered out onto the trail. He was staring at the pony in alarmed disorientation when he heard a moan behind him. He turned around carefully to avoid falling.

The warrior was getting up from the ground holding a bloody wound at the side of his head. Without thinking, Lion Hunter lurched into staggering action. The Blackfeet was raising his war club when Lion Hunter smashed his rock down on the warrior's shoulder. The blow jarred the war club free. A second powerful blow, this one to his enemy's forehead, sent the Blackfeet tumbling over backwards and the violence was over. The warrior lay still in an unmoving tangle of arms, legs, and twisted torso.

When the warrior did not move again, Lion Hunter slumped back against a nearby rock, energy spent and mind numbed. Without purpose, he let his eyes drift over the scene. When they came to rest, it was on the entrance to the marmot's burrow.

As calm slowly overtook his emotional shock, awareness of the real world crept back into him. The marmot's shadowed face stared back at him from the burrow, its nose twitching. Nearly trampled moments before, the creature was already back tending to the ongoing needs of its life, curiously investigating for new signs of danger. Lion Hunter smiled.

Thank you for saving me, little brother. And for reminding me this day is not yet over.

Awareness of the day's needs triggered, Lion Hunter looked over at the enemy warrior. Even in death the man was powerful looking—a thick bodied Blackfeet warrior, about twenty winters in age. Chunks of raw flesh hung from the calf of the man's right leg and jagged bone poked out of the open wound.

He was scraped form his pony when it crashed into the boulder.

"You attacked a man-brave," Lion Hunter muttered as he looked down at the fierce painting on the warrior's slack face. "I counted coup on you twice. I think maybe I am not only a man now but also a warrior." He scoffed at his bragging. He had no witness to testify to his achievement.

Switching his thoughts to the needs of the moment, Lion Hunter realized he was still holding the rock. He lifted his arm and looked at the rock. Hair was imbedded in the thickening blood that clung to it. Pushing himself away from the boulder, he tossed the rock downslope. Behind him, the warrior's pony snorted—Lion Hunter had forgotten it was there. He turned to look at it.

The pony stood facing him, ears forward, tail twitching.

You are nervous, aren't you, pretty one? Don't be, this battle is over.

The animal was beautiful, painted with a brilliant red war mask and seven white stick horse figures extending down over its front shoulder. Yellow circles were painted around two large scars on its rump—old battle wounds. The animal was also newly injured, though not seriously, its right shoulder and side scrapped from its first collision with the boulder. Luckily for the pony, the warrior's leg had absorbed most of the second impact.

Calmer now, Lion Hunter heard the shifting sounds of several more ponies from the Blackfeet's back-trail. He turned back around. A small heard of ponies stood in a crowded line on the path, many strides beyond the dead warrior, all facing the battle scene, watching intently. One nickered softly, and the war pony behind him answered.

Lion Hunter waited until his thoughts settled, then turned back toward the war pony. Suppressing a limp and speaking in soothing tones so the animal would not spook, he walked toward it. The animal was still nervous but probably wouldn't move farther away from its herd-mates along the narrow trail because there was no opportunity to circumvent Lion Hunter or otherwise return to the herd. Lion Hunter gently took hold of the pony's lead and began walking back toward his newly-won herd, but when he reached the warrior, the man unexpectedly began stirring.

Lion Hunter stopped, surprise penetrating the dullness of his mind. As he looked down the pony stretched its neck out and nuzzled against the Blackfeet's shoulder.

Still holding the pony's lead, Lion Hunter bent and picked up the warrior's elaborately decorated war club tossing it farther along the trail. He retrieved his own knife from the dirt, hiked his rear end up onto a rock, and sat looking down at the warrior.

The Blackfeet looked up into Lion Hunter's eyes, remaining defiantly silent.

Lion Hunter assessed the man's broken leg. He could not fight with that injury—he posed no further danger. They continued looking at one another in silence.

After a while, the warrior took a deep breath, and muscles taut, pulled himself to a sitting position, his back unwittingly covering the marmot's burrow. The Blackfeet looked briefly at his destroyed leg, then back up at Lion Hunter. There was no fear in him—he conceded nothing to his conqueror.

After a moment longer, Lion Hunter pointed his chin at the warrior's leg and signed.

"You, dead, maybe." The man was still many days from his people's land, and the injury was probably too serious for him to survive the long journey. Survival would probably not even be possible with help.

The warrior maintained his defiant look.

Not able to think of any purposeful thing to do with the warrior, Lion Hunter slipped down from the boulder and dropped the pony's lead in the dirt next to the Blackfeet.

Hiding his own concerns, Lion Hunter brazenly stepped over the Blackfeet's shattered leg and walked toward the remaining herd without turning back.

I think I am not only a man today, but with this battle, I am also a warrior. It does not matter that I have no witness to tell the truth of the battle to our elders. These ponies are my plunder, and my people will think I am a fine man when I bring them to our village.

Halfway to the bunched horses, Lion Hunter became overwhelmed by emotional exhaustion. He sat down cross-legged beside the path and, after a brief glance back to assure the Blackfeet could not attack again, took Fox's water skin from his pack. It was nearly empty, but he drank the last anyway. He needed a rest before turning the ponies around on the narrow trail and beginning the return trip to his village. The animals were still restless, so he decided to let them calm before moving any closer.

His wandering thoughts were forced back to the present by the sound of nervous hoof-steps.

It is the Blackfeet war-horse.

Sighing, he lifted his head and glanced back along the trail. The Blackfeet was standing one-legged on a calf-high rock. As Lion Hunter watched, he used his good leg to launch himself high enough to get his belly over the animal's back. From there, he grabbed the pony's mane and worked his good leg over its broad back. The gravely injured warrior forced himself upright and sat rigid for a moment, absorbing the pain of his movements in silence. Then, without looking back, the warrior urged his pony into a slow walk along the elk trail, continuing down the trail toward the talus slide. The warrior looked down at his war club, lying in the dirt, as he passed, but he did not stop.

You are right to leave that club. You will make no more war in the real world, I think. Have a good spirit journey.

Lion Hunter watched the pony pick its way through the talus-slide, becoming smaller and smaller until finally both rider and mount disappeared from sight.

He was still sitting, his head cradled in his arms, when he heard whimpering—like frightened puppy sounds. He looked back toward the talus-slide. No Blackfeet, no puppy.

Then, while returning the water skein to his pack, he heard the muffled whimper again. The unusual sound was curious, but he decided he would rest a little longer before investigating.

When he did rise and begin walking toward his new herd, he was relieved to find all were tethered together. He would not have to chase them. The lead pony was coal black, easily the largest horse Lion Hunter had ever seen. It was lashed to a stout bush, and backed as far away from Lion Hunter's approach as its lead allowed. He padded past the uneasy animal without acknowledging its presence. As he passed each of the others, he reached out and ran his hand along its body while speaking in respectful tones. He was congratulating himself on a successful introduction when he heard the whimper again. He was now sure it was a puppy.

He walked back to the third horse in the string, this time scratching the haunches of each as he passed. The sound was coming from a two-sided willow carrying pack draped over the pony's back.

He unlashed the lid and lifted it. He fell back astonished. A chubby wolf puppy cowered inside.

"I see the brave has become a man, and the man a warrior, all on this one day," a gravelly voice announced behind him just off the trail.

Lion Hunter flinched as lightning flashed through him. Beyond that, however, he had no strength to react. He leaned his forehead heavily against the basket and let out his breath. It was Spirit Man.

As the silence extended he began feeling wet laps to his nose and cheeks. He opened an eye—it was the pup. The little fur-ball was standing on its hind legs, paws against the inside of the pack, excitedly licking him. A calm flooded over the nerve-fires that had been ignited inside him by Spirit Man's unexpected greeting. Lion Hunter smiled.

Pushing himself upright, he turned and spoke.

"Hey, ya, Grandfather. I am a man today. Maybe, when those of the council see my plunder," he waved his hand, indicating the string of ponies, "they will declare me a warrior for my battle with the Blackfeet I counted coup on."

Lion Hunter gently lifted the wolf pup out of the pack and cuddled it to his chest as he watched Spirit Man climb up out of the bushes and onto the trail.

20

Spirit Man spoke. "I saw a Blackfeet warrior come by and leave these seven ponies here a small time back. I think maybe he mistook one Wolf Ridge man for easy prey. He looked very fierce, but he was not so smart, I think."

Despite his annoyance with the old man Lion Hunter flushed with pride.

"This pup is wolf," Spirit Man observed.

"Yes, and so is my spirit totem," Lion Hunter gushed, suddenly excited to brag about all that happened to him. "A wolf spirit vision came to me on the mountain. I will go to our holy man so he can tell me the messages of both."

Lion Hunter set his backpack on the ground and sat down beside it.

"You must tell me of these things."

Spirit Man took a bladder of water and some jerky from beneath his clothing and sat while Lion Hunter told him about all his quest adventures.

* * *

"And so this bear is dead?" Spirit Man asked when Lion Hunter had completed his tale.

"Yes," Lion Hunter responded, the word erupting from his mouth in the middle of a breath. He quickly reached into his backpack and pulled out one of the half-foots, holding it up for Spirit Man to see.

Spirit Man looked at the severed foot then, a moment later, shifted his eyes to Lion Hunter's, making neither facial expression nor comment.

"It is for the claws," Lion Hunter blurted, suddenly embarrassed by what strange things he imagined Spirit Man must be thinking.

Spirit Man nodded, picking up the water bladder from where Lion Hunter had set it.

"The flies and the vultures were thick," Lion Hunter added again.

Spirit Man lifted the bladder and took a drink.

"Grandfather," Lion Hunter suddenly remembered that many vultures waited while only one ate, "many vultures came but only one ate while the others waited. Why would they do that?"

Spirit Man took a second drink of water, tied it off, and returned the bladder to the ground at his side.

"Do you not use your think-habit now that you are a man?" he asked.

Lion Hunter flushed, ashamed of his failure.

"My thoughts are tired. It is like I have only smoke behind my eyes."

Spirit Man thought for a moment then cleared his throat.

"What is the difference between a vulture's prey and that of others?"

"The vulture eats only what is dead and smelly." Lion Hunter shrugged, his brow still furrowed.

"So they eat only what others do not want. Do you think there is need to hurry?"

Still not thinking clearly, Lion Hunter accepted the answer as all that the old man was going to say on the subject and rose to finish preparing for his journey back to the Wolf Ridge village. When he slung his pack over his shoulder and walked off toward the string of ponies, Spirit Man called after him, asking his intentions.

"You will travel to our village with all these ponies?"

"Yes," Lion Hunter answered over his shoulder, sounding more confident than he knew he should. Even traveling across his own people's land, a single man with so much plunder would be in danger of attack.

Maybe the Blackfeet was afraid I would see all his plunder and so he attacked me first.

"The Blackfeet lives?" Spirit Man pressed.

"Yes, but a splintered bone pokes from his leg. I think he will die before he comes to his people. I have counted coup on him in battle. Twice. His death is for the spirit fathers to decide."

Spirit Man nodded to Lion Hunter's back.

"I am only an old dead man, but my heart would sing with the wind if I could journey with our people's newest man and warrior."

"Thank you, Grandfather. You make me proud." Lion Hunter stopped and turned, looking at the old man gratefully. His return journey would be safe now—no enemy could ever sneak up on Spirit Man.

The narrow trail, where the Blackfeet left the ponies, skirted a cliff on one side, a drop off on the other. Lion Hunter put the pup down and began turning the seven horses around one at a time while the pup waddled around under foot. When all faced the right direction for his trip home, Lion Hunter returned to the hind-most, the black horse that had been tethered to bushes, and began stringing their leads together so that all could be easily led in an emergency. He was again struck by the giant size of the animal.

While Lion Hunter finished readying the ponies, the old man passed among them, scratching their rumps, feeding each a small bit of oats and speaking quietly into their ears. He stopped when he came to the giant and turned his eyes back to his younger companion.

Lion Hunter, seeing Spirit Man's odd expression, tied off the final lead and walked back to where the old man stood. Spirit Man's eyes shifted to the horse and Lion Hunter followed his gaze. Thick-knotted scar tissue stood out on the horse's right shoulder and upper leg—four claw marks raking downward, thick and deep at the top, shallower at the bottom.

I did not see this before. It is because I turned this pony around from its other side.

"Mountain lion," Lion Hunter stated flatly.

Spirit Man nodded.

"Carries-His-Lion, maybe has a twin," Spirit Man chortled, referring to the four lion-claw scars on the warrior chief's right shoulder and upper arm.

Nodding, Lion Hunter studied the rest of the animal. It was as tall at the withers as the top of Lion Hunter's head. It was also much more thickly muscled than the rest of the ponies in the string.

"This is the biggest pony I have ever seen, Grandfather. Have you known one so big?"

"Yes. It is like those of the hair-faces who live far from here." He pointed to the south. "When I journeyed there, many years ago, a desert man had one that he stole from other Indians, who stole it from the hair-faces."

"What are the hair-faces? Lion Hunter asked, pushing hair back from his own face.

"I never saw one so I know little of them. The desert man told me they have pale skin all over their bodies and long hair on their faces, except for their eyes, but he did not know where they came from, only that they had giant ponies."

Lion Hunter felt something soft pressing against his leg and looked down. The pup, standing on its hind legs with front paws against his leg, was smiling up at him. Mentally drifting away from the conversation about far-away people, his thoughts went back to the big pony and its scars. He picked up the pup and, holding it to his chest, walked away. A plot forming in his mind pulled up at the corners of his mouth.

That first day they traveled into the early afternoon. Lion Hunter was too exhausted to go any farther. Spirit Man left camp, calling back that he was going to get a rabbit. Lion Hunter, the new man-warrior, unloaded and hobbled each of the ponies then set them out to graze. The other side of the woven basket he'd found the wolf in contained more plunder, but he resisted sorting through it until he had prepared their camp.

While Grandfather roasted two rabbits over the campfire, Lion Hunter inspected the basket's remaining contents. There was dried venison, some pemmican—the latter tasted like sage and was not as good as that made by Lion Hunter's own people—the Blackfeet's fire-starting materials, leggings and his war paints. There was also a stunning buckskin shirt decorated with many strings of tiny blue/green bobbles. The bobbles were made of stone, but of a kind unfamiliar to him. Grandfather called the pebbles turquoise and said it came from the desert people. Lion Hunter held the shirt for a long while fingering its stitching as his thoughts made a picture of his mother, and he became quiet.

Spirit Man watched but said nothing.

There was also a mask made of dried twigs bound together by twine made from willow. The mask had huge red lips painted on it and, when he saw it, Spirit Man became excited. The mask reminded Lion Hunter of the story Spirit Man told him about a strangely dressed man with a mask who saved him from death long ago, before he was made dead by his own people. Lion Hunter remembered the strange man was the one who journeyed far from his own lands to see the great fish herds of the northwestern rivers.

The last thing he discovered was the strangest of all. It was a knife made of a strange material new to Lion Hunter. Spirit Man called the material 'metal.' It was shiny and much tougher than rock. It made a very strange sound when he struck it against rock.

"This is a mighty trophy," the old man told him. "Among our people, the man who possesses it will, I think, soon enjoy much importance. This is so wherever metal journeys. Metal also comes from the hair-faces."

The knife's blade was very sharp, not chipped or cracked like the bone and stone knives Lion Hunter knew. The handle was not lashed to the blade with rawhide either. There was a thin layer of wood on each side of the metal and all was fastened with small metal spikes somehow driven through both wood and metal, from one side to the other. Lion Hunter cut some wood with it to test its usefulness. He was fascinated with its heft and effectiveness. It was fine plunder.

* * *

The five-day journey back was uneventful, and Lion Hunter had lots of time to daydream and plan.

Lion Hunter knew he would be welcomed back into his village as a man. That was customary for all questing initiates. Counting coup upon an enemy warrior in battle, though, was not customary for a man-brave so he did not know how his people would react to that. Also, Lion

Hunter was returning to the village with a string of ponies and other valuable plunder after leaving on the journey with only a knife and a small pack.

He hoped a special council would be called and the village elders would believe his story about the battle. He hoped also that Willow's father would see his achievements with fresh eyes. But what excited him most were his daydreams of once again seeing Willow.

At one point, Spirit Man asked him what the young Crow warrior, Fox, told him when they signed after the bear's death. Lion Hunter relayed their conversations, but Grandfather seemed less interested after that and the subject did not come up again.

He and Spirit Man enjoyed playing with, and watching, the wolf cub's antics at night, and each day Lion Hunter carried the little guy close to him in a sling the old man made from reeds. He welcomed Spirit Man's help and company through out those five days, and was genuinely disappointed when the old man, as always, slipped off into the wilderness just before the Wolf Ridge village came into view.

Lion Hunter skirted the village, choosing to go to the pasturing fields first so he could leave most of his newly acquired wealth to graze. Several of the pasture boys rushed over to inspect his new herd and ask excited questions about how he managed to steal them. They were impressed that he completed his vision quest. They also wanted to know what thrilling adventures he had during his quest. All of them eyed the wolf pup in his arms but none asked about it directly. That would have been rude. Lion Hunter was honored by the youngsters' interest, but he told them such stories would have to wait until another time. He cut the huge black horse out before mingling the others with Kills-In-The-Dark's herd. Her lead mare would assert herself over the six new ones.

He rode off toward the village on the giant black, accompanied by several mounted pasture boys who continued to pepper him with excited questions.

He rode directly to his mentor's lodge, dismounting and calling out her name. The pasture boys peeled off, one by one, returning to their duties among the village herds.

"Ho, Aunt Kills-In-The-Dark, it is Hunter. I would speak to my favorite warrior and mentor."

"What young man is this that comes to my lodge and calls out my name?" her excited voice called back as she threw aside the teepee's entrance flap and rushed out to meet him.

Both had proud grins, him for her greeting and she for the joy his return brought to her.

"You make a fine man," she announced with hands on hips and serious tone as he slid off of the giant's shoulder.

She stood, looking him up and down, her one good eye finally coming to rest on the wolf pup. "Come, come inside. You must tell me all of your adventures since leaving," she said, glancing back at the giant black horse as she bent to enter.

Following her lead, Lion Hunter set the pup down on the ground and told it to 'stay' as he ducked through the lodge's entrance. The welcome smell of the teepee's interior washed over him and he breathed in deep savoring it while holding the flat of his hand out to prevent the pup from climbing in behind him. The minute-sized wolf stopped, looked over its shoulder for a moment, then—apparently satisfied nothing threatened it from that direction—sat staring after Lion Hunter with sad eyes.

Lion Hunter was ready to begin his story telling, but before he could start…

The heads are gone!

"Where are your trophies?" he spit out, too surprised to ask politely.

His mentor bowed her head, peeking up at him through hanging bangs. It was a self-conscious gesture—one he had never before seen in her.

"My thoughts grew burdened with the weight of those trophies. They were old and ugly to look at, and they begged always to be released so they could make their journey to the spirit world. Besides," she continued, raising her head and squaring her shoulders, "I have you to make worries about now."

Lion Hunter's heart thumped. He cleared his throat before speaking.

"I have made my vision quest and conquered a fierce Blackfeet warrior who attacked me." He smiled at the astonishment in her surprised expression. "I return with seven horses and other plunder, and I hope soon to be recognized as a warrior by council."

Kills-In-The-Dark sat silent, looking at him, her good eye wet with a beginning tear.

"I think I have two mothers now," Lion Hunter quickly continued, reaching across and laying his hand on her legging-covered knee, "one who is gone but still in my heart and another who entered my heart and stayed to make me a proud warrior."

She clutched his hand in both of hers, holding it tightly to her knee as tears washed down over the scarred tissue of the face he'd come to know and treasure.

"When I make my lodge, I will invite you to live with Willow and I. We will have a fine two-warrior lodge," he announced with pride.

When she hesitated, he quickly added, "Without you I would miss the sweet smell of your lodge. And also, we will always camp next to your husband's teepee—it is the right thing to do."

He shifted, sitting up to his full height, thrusting out his chin and looking every bit the dignified warrior.

She smiled up at him full of pride, snuffling and wiping her cheek dry with her sleeve.

They talked quietly for a short while longer, him telling her of his adventures, but after a bit she reminded him that Willow would discover his return and would be sad if he did not go to see her soon.

Lion Hunter asked if he could leave the pup with her for a short while. At her direction, he lifted the little guy into the teepee and handed him to her.

Outside, Lion Hunter flung himself up on the giant black stallion's thickly muscled back, but before he could kick the animal into action Kills-In-The-Dark came out of her teepee holding the pup and waving for him to wait. She walked up to the stallion and ran her hand over the scarred claw marks, penetrating eye bright with understanding.

"A chief must feel respected before he can be led," she said and stepped back from the horse.

As he rode away she called after him, "You are my pretty warrior, Lion Hunter."

* * *

He rode the stallion proudly through the middle of camp. Upon coming to Carries-His-Lion's teepee, he dropped to the ground.

"Uncle, it is Lion Hunter, I ask to speak with you about a good thing." He addressed the Warrior Chief as uncle, to be respectful.

"What do you want, boy?" The indolent words drifted from behind the lodge entrance's closed flap.

"I have found your horse," Lion Hunter announced, standing away so the warrior would get a full view of the animal's stunning beauty.

He knew what he said would be senseless to the War Chief who had lost no horses—that was his plan. The message was carefully designed, its provocative idea rehearsed repeatedly during the past five days of travel.

After making the statement, he stood quietly, hoping the plan would work.

Rousing sounds broke the silence from inside, and, a moment later, the entrance-flap was pulled back. The chief of the Lion Shadows, still sitting, was leaning toward the entrance so he could look up to see Lion Hunter.

His eyes flitted over Lion Hunter before shifting to the stunningly handsome stallion and going wide with surprise. He reacted too quickly to maintain any real dignity, but as soon as he got outside he visibly calmed himself before casually beginning an examination of the largest horse he had ever seen. The horse stood, looking back at him, proud, self-confident and aloof, towering over the chief.

"Look at the other side, Uncle. I am sure this pony is yours," Lion Hunter said, eyeing the old claw scars on the chief's shoulder and arm.

Carries-His-Lion eyed Lion Hunter a moment longer to assure he was not being made a fool of.

Lion Hunter held his breath, waiting in silence. He watched the chief's bare feet beneath the horse's belly, as they padded around the horse's far side and came to an abrupt halt. After a moment, the War Chief's fingers came into view, tracing a line over the scar tissue on the horse's withers.

When Carries-His-Lion finished his inspection, he returned to stand in front of Lion Hunter, looking puzzled.

"Uncle, I took this proud animal from a Blackfeet I counted coup on while returning from my quest. When I saw the marks on its shoulder, I knew it was sent from the spirit world as a gift to you, and I could not keep it. I have brought this spirit pony to you. I am only the messenger of our Spirit Fathers." His voice trailed off at the end.

Carries-His-Lion looked at him a moment longer, then broke into a broad smile. The warrior chief was filling his chest with air as though about to speak when a look of shock swept the smile away. He backed toward his teepee, and Lion Hunter's thoughts scrambled.

What have I done? How can he not like this fine pony?

The chief turned and ducked back inside his lodge with alarming swiftness. Lion Hunter heard frantic movements inside, one thing after another clearly being flung to the earth. He stood frozen.

Finally, all sound from inside stopped and Lion Hunter heard the chief exhale, as though relieved. When he exited next, he carried his war shield, a beautifully detailed disk of the thickest buffalo skin available, taken from the animal's hump, smoke-hardened, painted and draped with long hanks of buffalo hair around its edges. Lion Hunter saw it many times as the chief proudly rode out of camp on raids against their enemy, holding it high for all to see.

"You take. Gift," the chief said soberly poking it out at arm's length toward Lion Hunter.

Lion Hunter realized that the chief, having been presented the horse as a gift, felt obliged to respond with a gift of his own. When Lion Hunter did not accept it immediately the chief withdrew it and pumped it back out at arm's length, again saying, "You take."

Lion Hunter reluctantly reached his hand toward the shield but pulled it back at the last moment.

"Uncle, it is not I who gives this gift to you. It is the Spirit Fathers. I do not feel worthy of this fine shield you so generously offer to me, but I will take it if you allow me to make my own gift to you. Will you do that?"

Carries-His-Lion squinted at Lion Hunter, suspicion etched into his face.

He continued watching as Lion Hunter reached beneath his shirt and pulled out the metal knife. Lion Hunter turned the knife's handle toward the chief and extended it, taking hold of the shield with his other hand. He watched as the warrior chief's fingers closed around the handle—as he stroked both blade and handle, then hefted the weapon it in his hand.

When the proud War Chief of the Lion Shadow society looked up he was wearing a huge grin.

"It is a good trade, and you are a fine messenger for the Spirit Fathers." The chief walked back over to the big stallion and ran his hand over the rippling muscles of its chest.

"Uncle, I was attacked by a Blackfeet who was painted in fierce war paint and on the war path. Because I was returning from my vision quest, I had no weapon and had to fight him with a rock…"

"Did you strike him?" Carries-His-Lion's hand stopped stroking as he lifted his head to look quizzically at Lion Hunter.

"Yes, Uncle. Twice."

"Then a council must be called so all can know you are now a warrior."

There is hope for you, my fine War Chief. Thank you.

Lion Hunter faked an innocent look of surprise.

"What should I do? I cannot call a council."

"I will go now and call for a council myself." The War Chief grabbed a hank of the stallion's mane and slung himself up on its back. Lion Hunter watched as he trotted off toward the camp chief's teepee. He had never seen Carries-His-Lion look so proud.

Lion Hunter was still congratulating himself when the thick warrior turned back to him, and gave a friendly wave, wearing that uncommonly broad smile.

When the Carries-His-Lion was safely out of sight, Lion Hunter sprinted for the herd pasture. He quickly located Black Storm, mounted him, gathered two of his remaining six ponies, and set off for Willow's teepee.

Riding through the village he looked for, and found, the huge black stallion he'd given Carries-His-Lion. It stood in front of Chief Weasel Bear's teepee. A moment later, Lion Hunter dropped to the ground before Willow's lodge.

He tethered the two specially selected ponies to her father's picket, beside the sag-backed hand-me-down pony that was already there. The three greeted each other.

Willow's mother peeked from behind the entrance flap, and Lion Hunter greeted her.

"Aunt, it is a fine warm day. I wish to speak to your husband, the brave warrior, Stone Shirt." His words came out more awkwardly than planned, but he was so nervous he did not know how to correct it without sounding dumb. Instead, he watched Willow's mother silently staring at the two horses tethered to their lodge picket. After a moment, she ducked back inside and the entrance flap was pulled close. There was a muffled conversation and a brief pause before Stone Shirt finally emerged, pulling his shirt down over his head. He eyed the two ponies while Lion Hunter cleared his throat.

At that moment the camp caller came running by announcing that a special council was to be held and that Lion Hunter was being called to attend. No timing could have been better. Lion Hunter smiled his most friendly smile.

"Uncle Stone Shirt, I must go to camp council now, but I gift these two fine ponies to you. I won them in battle with a Blackfeet warrior. I will soon be back so I can speak to you about taking your daughter, Willow, as my wife."

He saw Willow peeking out from the dark interior of the teepee smiling, and he smiled back.

* * *

Carries-His-Lion was waiting outside the camp chief's lodge, still smiling, when Lion Hunter rode up. Camp youngsters were already gathering in excited knots, wondering why the sudden council was called. Others, both warriors and wives, also began arriving.

Lion Hunter, chest puffed, slid from Black Storm's shoulder and strutted up to Carries-His-Lion, who immediately threw his arm around the young man-brave's shoulder and escorted him inside the camp chief's teepee.

The other four chiefs were already sitting circled around the lodge fire. A space large enough for both of them had been left open. Carries-His-Lion, smiling, sat and gestured to the space, next to him.

"Sit," he invited.

Lion Hunter sat.

He had daydreamed about this moment many times during the days and nights of his return journey, but those fantasies had not prepared him for the overwhelming shock of actually being brought before a council of his people's most respected elders. He sat, mute, not knowing what else to do.

There were five chiefs in the circle, all—except Carries-His-Lion—solemnly looking at him. Crow Chaser nodded to him and he nodded back, letting his eyes fall away after that brief greeting because he was embarrassed to be sitting among their gathered importance.

Weasel Bear's wife handed her husband his sacred pipe and, while the rest sat silently watching, he removed it from its elk skin cover, assembled bowl to stem, tamped it with tobacco, and lit it.

The pipe was passed around the circle, each chief performing the same blessing ritual in silence—blowing and fanning the potent talisman's cleansing smoke out to the six corners of the earth before passing it on.

Like all young braves, Lion Hunter had sneaked off to smoke crumbled grass through makeshift bone pipes. But this was different. Today, Lion Hunter was being acknowledged as a guardian of his people, the single-most powerful ceremonial experience in the life of a Wolf Ridge male.

As Lion Hunter waited nervously for the pipe to make its way around the circle, his chest became tight and he could hardly breath. He took shallow breaths, hoping the others would not notice how humbled he was by his inclusion in the ceremony.

After his turn, Carries-His-Lion extended the pipe to Lion Hunter, holding it out to him at arm's length. The young man-brave's hands shook so violently he fumbled and nearly dropped it.

Lion Hunter's fingers tingled where they touched the powerful talisman and when, at long last, he drew in its sacred smoke, lighting flashed through him and, in his mind, he swooped with stomach twisting acrobatics high up over the world.

No previous experience in his lifetime, not even facing the furious bear on Wolf Ridge, impacted his being so powerfully. Portentous spirits whirled around him, plunged into his chest, and careened thorough his insides, and through all, Lion Hunter imagined himself standing, feet imbedded in rock, ready to defend his people against all threat.

He became dizzy, taking great gulping breaths as he tried to concentrate on the faraway sounds of the council voices. He squinted his eyes, both hands flat on the ground beside him, arm muscles straining. Weasel Bear now held the pipe and was speaking to the others. Lion Hunter couldn't remember passing it to him.

Then, Carries-His-Lion was speaking.

"...and his pony ran over Lion Hunter, knocking his knife away, and him from the trail. But Lion Hunter leaped back to the trail and attacked the fierce Blackfeet warrior, smashing him twice with a rock, the only weapon he could find. And when he finished this battle, he left the Blackfeet broken—a no-more warrior lying in the dirt. So, while the no-more warrior watched," Carries-His-Lion put his hand on Lion Hunter's shoulder and squeezed, "Lion Hunter robbed this Blackfeet of seven horses and other fine plunder. Does this not make our man-brave into a warrior?"

Each of the chiefs nodded in turn, smiling briefly at Lion Hunter before turning their attention back to Chief Weasel Bear.

"Lion Hunter," the camp chief said, "you bring much pride to our people with this victory over our enemy. Your people recognize this coup you have counted upon the Blackfeet. I think Carries-His-Lion makes a gift to you now."

Surprised, Lion Hunter turned to Carries-His-Lion not knowing what to expect.

The Lion Shadow chief held out his open hand, a single eagle tail feather lay on it. The warrior chief was grinning like a proud mother. Lion Hunter smiled back, lifting the feather reverently from the other's palm. After an awkward moment of embarrassment, he stood and poked it down into the hair at the back of his head.

"Go, young warrior," Weasel Bear prompted, "show our people who protects the women and children of our village now."

Lion Hunter stood, pulled back the entrance flap, and, stepping out into the open, stood up straight. He looked around at the crowd, selecting various warriors and older women to grace with the dignified nod of a warrior.

Willow's mother was there, but neither Willow, nor her father was. Kills-In-The-Dark stood off several steps, holding Black Storm's bridle, watching. Pony Man stood with her.

Lion Hunter strode over and took the bridle rope from his second mother.

"Lion Hunter," it was Pony Man, "I would learn the story of your quest and your battle with the Blackfeet. It is a story that needs to be told around the village campfire."

Lion Hunter nodded to him.

I know a secret about you. Spirit Man has a partner in black-rock trading with my new Crow friend and his village.

The new warrior stood quietly, now looking at Kills-In-The-Dark. Those surrounding them fell into silence. Finally, Lion Hunter spoke.

"Second mother, I will always provide for you and when my lodge is built, I will be proud to welcome you there for all time." Even she was surprised when he bent and kissed her on the forehead.

* * *

Lion Hunter rode up to Willow's lodge, his heart bursting with pride.

"Uncle Stone Shirt, I wish to take Willow as my wife," he called out, stopping in front of the teepee.

After a long pause, the man's voice asked, "Who is this that comes to my lodge calling out for the whole village to hear?"

So the cold in your lodge is not all your wife's.

"Uncle, I meant no disrespect. It is only that I am now a warrior, and I am anxious to… I want to…" Panicked, he couldn't think of anything to say beyond that—he hadn't thought beyond Willow and he becoming husband and wife.

"Beaver Tail wants to take my Willow as his second wife," Willow's father said, not bothering to come out of the teepee.

"But, Uncle, I have already given you two fine ponies." Lion Hunter's embarrassed panic became fearful panic.

"I think Beaver Tail might give three."

"I will give four," Lion Hunter snapped back. He hoped the remaining two would be enough to trade for the buffalo skins he needed to make a lodge.

"I do not see these others Do you think to trick me?" Still, Stone Shirt hid in the darkness of his lodge.

"I am a warrior now, I am honorable." Lion Hunter was becoming annoyed.

"How do I know they are not sway backed or splay footed if I do not see them?"

Lion Hunter paused, pressing back the urge to become angry.

"I saw Beaver Tail and his wife together as I rode here. I think that I will go now to ask *them* if he means to take a second wife." He was taking a chance in making the threat, but he didn't think Beaver Tail's wife would enjoy having another woman in their lodge. She already had a sister, a mother, and a mother-in-law to complicate her life.

"I guess you make a fair gift offer, but do you have a lodge for my precious Willow to live in?" His answer was too quick. Lion Hunter smelled victory. His heart soared.

"Splay-footed ponies are safer to ride because they do not move so fast, and it is easier to mount a pony that is a little sway backed." Lion Hunter, now sure of himself, teased the retired warrior.

"Enough, I will not bicker. My daughter's happiness is all that matters. Willow will come with you now to fetch my two other ponies."

Willow came bursting out of the teepee and ran up to Black Storm's side. After an awkward moment, she stretched her arm out for him to help her up behind him on Black Storm. He responded instantly and they rode off, her, hugging him close from behind, him, proudly looking straight ahead.

He rode the long way through their village pretending not to see all the surprised and admiring looks they attracted.

I am a warrior, and I have my Willow as wife! My heart rides with the wind.

Made in the USA
San Bernardino, CA
13 December 2018